I0714530

"Jennifer Lewis writes for those who blink and find ourselves face to face with the tender realities of adulthood—the parts about growing up and being in the world that nobody ever warns us about: How lonely it can be and what the hell we're supposed to do about it.

It hurts to be here for Lewis' characters. They harbor a deep, lonely nostalgia as they navigate through their current moment; as if they've left their best and useful traits behind at a bar next to that one sweatshirt, and now it's cold. But story after story, Lewis reminds us that the way we remedy the unresolvable ache is to move toward one another; and, what we cannot fix within is actually the grace that brings and holds us together though the worst of it. All we have is one another, exactly what we need.

With embodied and incisive prose, Lewis zooms into the moments where we catch ourselves becoming human. She spotlights the singularity of universal experiences—watching a loved one slip away, losing control of bodily agency, feeling at once not enough and too much—and takes us to the place where empathy blooms."

CHRISTINE NO
author of *Whatever Love Means*

"The stories in Jennifer Lewis' *The New Low* are compelling, surprising, yet utterly recognizable. So much of what it means, and feels like, to be human is captured in this stunning collection. The small worries, the large catastrophes, new birth, and impending death, all find their moment. A fascination with larger-than-life characters takes a disillusioning hit as the curtain is pulled back and the unraveling begins. And yet, for all the exposing of what lies beneath the surface, there is a consistent and profound sympathy for the human condition itself. And no one is exactly a stranger in these vivid, wrenching, and beautiful stories, because the honesty and skill in the writing, reminds us that we too are of their kind."

PETER BULLEN
author of *Wallflower*

WWW.NOMADICPRESS.ORG

MASTHEAD

FOUNDING PUBLISHER
J. K. Fowler

ASSOCIATE EDITOR
Michaela Mullin

DESIGN
Jevohn Tyler Newsome

MISSON STATEMENT Through publications, events, and active commun[ity]
participation, Nomadic Press collectively weaves together platforms fo[r]
intentionally marginalized voices to take their rightful place within the
world of the written and spoken word. Through our limited means, we a[re]
simply attempting to help right the centuries' old violence and silencing
that should never have occurred in the first place and build alliances an[d]
community partnerships with others who share a collective vision for a
future far better than today.

INVITATIONS Nomadic Press wholeheartedly accepts invitations to rea[d]
your work during our open reading period every year. To learn more or
extend an invitation, please visit: www.nomadicpress.org/invitations

DISTRIBUTION
Orders by teachers, libraries, trade bookstores, or wholesalers:

Nomadic Press Distribution
orders@nomadicpress.org
(510) 500-5162

Small Press Distribution
spd@spdbooks.org
(510) 524-1668 / (800) 869-7553

This book was made possible by a loving community of chosen family and friends, old and new.

For author questions or to book a reading at your bookstore, university/school, or alternative establishment, please se[nd]
an email to info@nomadicpress.org.

Cover art: Sarah Farrell

Artist portrait by Arthur Johnstone

Published by Nomadic Press, 1941 Jackson Street, Suite 20, Oakland, CA 94612

First printing, 2022

Library of Congress Cataloging-in-Publication Data

Title: *The New Low*
p. cm.
Summary: Like a hanging mobile, the stories in *The New Low* move around each other, creating ever-changing insights
between its characters. Each of whom struggle with identity, addictions, judgments, and life's contradictions.

[1. FICTION / Short Stories (single author). 2. FICTION / Women. 3. FICTION / General.]

LIBRARY OF CONGRESS CONTROL NUMBER: 2022941638

ISBN: 978-1-955239-32-5

THE
NEW
LOW

THE NEW LOW

STORIES BY **JENNIFER LEWIS**

NOMADIC PRESS

Oakland · Philadelphia · Xalapa

CONTENTS

FOREWORD

When I met Jennifer Lewis at San Francisco State, I was a *poet*. In *grad school*. Search those words together on the internet and you're sure to score screenshots of sketch characters from *Portlandia*. In comparison, Jennifer rocked these fabulous wide-brimmed hats and sassy monochrome jumpsuits, and entered a room like a breeze followed her.

Now mind you, I'm as gay as Liberace fisting Lindsey Graham with a glitter-encrusted plaster cast of Madonna's *Blonde Ambition* ponytail, so my observation wasn't of the creeper sort. I just thought: *Could this cool specimen really be a writer?* She seemed so put together.

Then I read her submissions in workshop—irreverent, in equal parts funny and sad, characters savoring and stewing in the muck of contemporary existence—and I thought, *Ah! She's a mess, too! We're all a mess!* A clown scarf of people dwelled within her, and I greedily pulled a new layer each time we hung out.

Early in our friendship, Jennifer asked me to read for her series, *Red Light Lit*, a performance salon on gender, love, and sexuality that has now become a beloved fixture in the San Francisco lit scene. I asked her what the tone for the series was, and she said "a little like Vaudeville," which I mistook for bawdy. When I apologized for my indiscretion, Jennifer shrugged her right shoulder—just her right shoulder—and gave me the most innocent-sounding snicker you've ever heard, and said, "It's cool. You were great."

The New Low evokes that same gesture—a sexiness, a messiness, an ease—with the language, with the characters: a wink, a single-shoulder shrug, and above all, a kindness despite the odds. The book does not try to perform linguistic somersaults. It uses the language of our lived experience—confusion, forgiveness, understanding—suggesting to *Look at who we are, look at what we do.* We marvel at what we see, and recognize it within ourselves. And that is why it is so damn good.

We all have seen, lived with and loved variations of Mae, Emma, Tanya, and definitely, Jonathan. Hell, I dated in Los Angeles during the opening act of the millennium; Jonathan's mommy issues are about as common as accidents on the 100 freeway, and equally difficult not to stare at with fascination. Emma's complicated acceptance of her evolving life could be the story of anyone's bestie. Mae is your neoliberal fantasy of success looked upon for too long, after the spotlight dies. But don't get it twisted—Lewis' characters are not archetypes. They are uniquely familiar and calamitous, and that makes them irresistible. It is a deft balance, and one that Lewis slays.

What *The New Low* explores most evocatively, however, is womanhood and motherhood—two identities strangely viewed as both mundane and extraordinary, and always deserving of a story. Again, a deft balance. In our culture there are writers and there are mothers. And though so many women out there are both, the two identities are presented as exclusive, hardly ever conflated in the public consciousness, as if one contradicts the other. How many women/mothers/writers must contend with this obtuse perspective? We often discuss writing as inhabiting the cracks in our world. Well, why not explore the cracks in womanhood? Motherhood? Such a vulnerability. And yet, we need to be reminded that these identities are not monolithic. To be a mother— to be a woman, for that matter—must you play a clown scarf of roles?

Lewis seems to ask this question, among others, in *The New Low*, with her inviting wink and laugh.

Miah Jeffra
author of *The Violence Almanac*

INTRODUCTION

Human relationships have always intrigued me; how they seem to ignite and thrive in liminal spaces, then extinguish or transform into something else. The fifteen stories in *The New Low* examine how relationships can be vital, as well as vortices of doom. I've been lucky enough to experience them as both, and wouldn't be the same person or writer without them. These stories were written at a time of quiet desperation. Having three children in the span of five years kept me homebound with a hunger for artistic collaboration, and with an ever changing body the world seemed comfortable commenting on constantly. Cognitively disconnected from others' perceptions of me, I felt objectified in an entirely new way. Pregnancy, birth, motherhood, and breastfeeding became an existential experience; yet, the culture and conversations around them reduced them to a stereotyped domesticity. Throughout the collection, literature and film as a means of intellectual, artistic, and social connection are common threads weaving in and out of conversations.

These stories were written to stand alone, but they are connected and arc as a novel. Regardless if you read this book from beginning to end or jump around, you will meet some recurring characters, as they move through time, spanning two decades, and various versions of themselves. *The New Low* explores what happens when people cling to youth and beauty, hide their secret addictions, and compartmentalize motherhood. Each of us experience interpersonal crises in one way or another, and I believe our personal revelations shine light on conflicts, hypocrisies, and joys of the human condition.

Jennifer Lewis

PUT A TEAT IN IT!

It tugs at my nipple. Only the first pull is uncomfortable, then it finds its rhythm. I hold the plastic horn against my breast with my forearm so I can use both hands to smoosh my left breast into the other horn. I shrink from the first suck, then feel the release of the swelling under my skin. I'm holding plastic gramophones to my breasts, but no music is coming out, only milky water drips into bottles that are screwed to them.

Put a sock in it! Originates from the gramophone. Put a breast in it! I think as my nipples are being suctioned down their skinny necks. I can see the pink flesh elongating, then contracting. Long plastic tubes connect the gramophones to an electronic box that's covered with black nylon so it can double as a backpack. It fools no one. Sitting on my nightstand, it echoes like a steam engine from another era. It starts off like *Choo-Choo*, Choo-Choo, but ten minutes in, it sounds more like *Fuck-You, Fuck-You.* I listen to it in unison with the suctioning while I wait for the 8-ounce bottles to fill.

When my husband barges in the room all I can say is, "Noooooooooh."

"I've seen it all," he says lightly as he looks for his keys or his hat. Ordinary things. No you haven't. You've only seen me with one gramophone under my shirt, not shirtless with both teats attached. Get out! I'm the one stuck here. Give me some dignity. I close my eyes. The industrial sound makes me feel like I'm in a factory. I am the factory. I start to leave my body. I'm always leaving my body. I notice that I leave so I tell myself, *Come back. Feel animal. Feel mammal. Feel cow.*

In 1920, the first mechanical breast pump was modeled after the bovine milking machine and little has changed about it since.

"Seriously, get out of here," I say.

"I'm not looking," he replies, moving papers around his desk. And I wonder how do you go back to woman after cow? Why is cow so scary? Maybe it's because you realize: You are something other than you think you are. What else am I that I don't already know?

"Found them!" He says, running out of the room.

O YOUTH AND BEAUTY!

Mae and I were sitting in the garden at the Chateau Marmont. It was dark and we were the only hotel guests outside when she asked, "Have you ever thought about hiring a professional?" A handful of hotel employees broke down a large white tent, moved wicker chairs, blew out hurricane candles, and carried trays of empty glasses into the hidden kitchen. Mae had so many people working for her that she could've been referring to a life coach, an ayahuasca shaman, or an assassin.

"Like a hit man?" I teased, remembering a story Mae told me years ago. Every day when she heard her husband's car drive up the gravel driveway, her stomach sank because something *hadn't* happened to him. I envisioned her behind an embroidered curtain, one eye peering out the window, everything she thought she wanted behind her: the waterfront home framed by Italian Cypresses, the modern interior with an 18th century nod to her South Carolina upbringing, a husband who read the newspaper in the morning and wore a blue suit to the office, and the extra rooms for children and a live-in nanny.

"You've never had a one-night stand," Mae said. "You don't know how exciting it can be with a stranger."

"It's never appealed to me," I replied, watching Oscar bus the table. He, like everyone else who worked at the hotel, looked like a soap opera star: tan skin, white teeth, and black hair that fell right into his green eyes. When he caught me staring at him, my cheeks flushed and I looked at Mae.

"I brought $1,000 with me, and I'm considering calling a gigolo," she said.

"I think they're called escorts now," I joked, until I realized that she was serious. "Mae, times are *not* that tough. You're a woman! You can sleep with people for free. Maybe even Oscar." I smiled at Oscar. He smiled back. "But by the looks of him, he probably has a girlfriend."

"I want a professional," she said, "because I don't want STIs, and no one could ever find out."

"Are you two okay?" Oscar walked up holding two glasses of champagne.

"Yes, great," I said. "Thanks for letting us stay. It's so nice to sit outside without a jacket."

"Where are you ladies from?"

"San Francisco," I said. "She lives in Malibu."

"We're here for a sort of celebration," Mae said.

"Well then," he placed the glasses on the table. "Don't get up and hug me or anything, but these are on me."

"Thank you," I said.

"You don't have to do that," Mae insisted. "At least let us give you a tip." She reached for her purse.

"Don't insult me." Oscar smiled and his dimples appeared. "If you two need anything, just let me know."

"Oh, we will," I said, peering at Mae.

"Anyway," Mae continued her thought before Oscar was out of ear shot and as an older gentleman walked in carrying a London newspaper, "if I'm having a one night stand I want to do it with someone who knows what they're doing, and I'm assuming that you wouldn't go into the business unless you had a big dick and knew how to get me off."

My eyes darted around and I politely smiled at the man with the newspaper. He wore expensive clothing: gray slacks, green cashmere sweater, and shiny shoes. He had a shaved baldhead with black stubbles except for a very deep widow's peak that shone in the darkness. He sat close enough to us that we couldn't continue our conversation. I was relieved. Instead, we talked about Mae's company she'd just sold.

Mae could sell anything but, like me, she didn't know a lot about business. She hired a finance guy, a marketing guru, and a social media intern, while she focused all of her energy on her product and customer service, and now she had a small online fashion empire. However, she lived in a constant state of disbelief and defensiveness. She worked incessantly. She barely saw her husband or her son. And her eyes started welling up as she talked about how much guilt she felt for leaving her toddler at home with the nanny.

"I just can't do this anymore," she said. "I feel like I'm on the verge of a nervous breakdown."

As she spoke, I began to notice a pulse underneath her left eye, and I attempted to make her laugh. "Maybe you could go to a place where they roll you out to sea with a blanket on your lap and you stare absentmindedly at the water for a month of recovery." Her face did not change. Her left eye twitched. "You know, one of those New Age religious retreats like Julianne Moore in *Safe*?"

"Those places are for housewives," she snapped.

"You mean, like me?" I said, waiting for her to say, You're not a housewife.

"Exactly," she replied.

I pulled my elbows off the table. I would never identify with the term housewife, and I couldn't believe Mae considered me as such. We sat looking offended at each other until she screamed, "I think I'm fucking up my kid! I can't stop working. I'm addicted to my phone. I don't sleep. My adrenal glands are shot. I don't even exercise anymore. Everyone expects me to fail. Even my husband secretly wants me to so I can be the wife that he's always wanted."

"*Jesus*, Mae. He married you. He knew what he was getting himself into."

"Did he? Did you? Does anyone?"

"Good point," I said.

"My son likes his nanny more than me, because she plays with him. When he was younger, I couldn't get to work fast enough. I didn't know what to do with a baby. Now that he's three, I want to play with him, but they have their routine and I just disrupt it. It's like he's happy until he sees me, and then he starts crying and throwing a tantrum. It's like, his life is better without me."

"That's not true." I reached across the table and held her hand.

"I honestly don't know how you do it," she said, "stay home with three kids." And for a moment I felt validated, and I basked in the compliment, until she removed her hand and placed an imaginary gun to her head and shot it. "I would die without using my brain."

I leaned back into the garden and listened to the traffic roaring down Sunset Boulevard. I took a breath and an image of Sylvia Plath appeared (or was it Gwyneth Paltrow playing Sylvia Plath?). She sat on a plaid blanket, a toddler next to her, an infant on her lap, a cool insanity burning from her eyes, and I remembered the pink tulips my husband—who had never read Sylvia Plath—handed me after my cesarean birth. The flowers sucked all the oxygen out of the room. My mother stood there holding my daughter. My silent ambivalence masked behind a smile.

"Goddamn, *Safe* is a brilliant movie," I said. "I wish I'd written that movie."

"That's going to be me," Mae replied. "I'm going to end up in an airtight room, sucking in oxygen…"

"Allergic to your affluent lifestyle brand!"

"Fuck you," she said, and this time we both laughed.

But then I noticed the corners of her mouth had turned white as if all the saliva had run out. "Maybe you *should* get some help?"

"That's my problem. I have too much help. I have a nanny, a babysitter, a housekeeper, a gardener, an assistant, an intern, a therapist, a nutritionist."

"Just like the movie," we said in unison.

"When we met, you were writing all the time." Mae lit a cigarette.

"I read now," I replied.

"I remember when you wanted to have five."

"Yeah, I did say that once. Three is plenty."

"I haven't read in years."

"I know. That's so strange. That was *our* thing. You know what I've been reading lately? Cheever's journals! Have you read them? They are exquisitely bleak, blissfully suicidal."

"Excuse me," the bald gentleman interrupted, "but I couldn't help noticing that you two are alone and was wondering if I could buy you ladies a drink."

No. Please go away. We were just talking about something interesting.

"You don't have to buy us a drink," Mae said.

"I'd like to," he replied.

Of course you do, but I'd like to talk to my friend about literature, and I need to have this conversation more than I need to know that I am still desirable.

"I insist," he continued.

"You must be staying at the hotel," Mae said.

"Yes. I've recently moved in."

"A hell of a place to live," Mae replied.

"Yeah, it's not too shabby," he said.

We introduced ourselves and Neil explained how he was recently divorced, sold his house in London, and had lived at the hotel for the last three months. He name-dropped that Tom Ford had put a bid on his house but someone outbid even him. He'd almost gone with the lower price, just to sell it to Ford.

"I loved the liberties he took with Isherwood's *A Single Man*," I said. "That script should've been nominated for Best Adapted Screenplay."

"Can I see a photo of it?" Mae grabbed Neil's phone.

While Mae marveled over the décor and architecture (houses and interiors didn't interest me much), I talked to Oscar, who walked over to say hello to Neil.

"Have you seen *A Single Man*?" I asked Oscar.

"Yeah, it's great. It was shot in 21 days."

"Was it? Have you read the book?"

"It's a book?"

"Yes, a great one by Christopher Isherwood. He lived in Hollywood. Influenced Truman Capote. You know, *Breakfast at Tiffany's*."

"Ohhh!" Oscar said. "There's a scene in the movie where George's lover, what was his name?"

"Jim," Mae said, still flicking through Neil's phone.

"When Jim's reading *Breakfast at Tiffany's*." Oscar's excitement radiates. "Ford must've done that strategically."

"He does everything strategically," Neil replied, as if he, too, was a man who did everything strategically. "He's a genius. I should've sold my house to him. I would have, if this divorce wasn't bleeding me."

Oscar and I gave each other a "must-be-nice" look while Mae and Neil talked about things that we could never afford. Oscar told us his friend was DJing at Bar Marmont and that we should walk down there. Mae and I agreed, and Neil said he had some business to take care of, but he would walk down a little later.

Most of the people at the Bar Marmont were young and desperately thin with bright, hungry eyes searching the room for celebrities or anyone with the power to make them famous. They looked twice at Mae. She often got mistaken for Jennifer Connelly, or sometimes Courtney Cox—she looked nothing like them in her youth, but she'd almost aged into them. Her round face became more narrow and angular, and the Botox in her forehead gave her that uniformed look. When the crowd realized we weren't anyone special, they melted back into their conversations. The music inside the bar was mostly hip hop, which Mae loved and I didn't, so I pulled back, hoping to grab a table outside the covered patio, where you could still smoke.

I watched Mae nodding her head to the bass, tall and striking, six thick bracelets on her right arm, wearing a dress of her own design. It was shapeless and beige, but showed her legs and high-heeled oxford shoes. I found myself wondering if she had a thousand dollars in her purse or was it still in the room? She couldn't possibly PayPal an escort, could she? A table opened up outside and I grabbed it, ordered a drink, and smoked while looking at all the unfulfilled faces and wondered if I looked unfulfilled too? Then Oscar walked in the door, all bright and hopeful with his dimples, and I gave him a hug. He sat down and when his drink arrived he said, "Thanks for keeping me company. My girlfriend is stuck in traffic."

"Of course!" I said, my heart deflating. "How long have you two been together?"

"Three months," he replied.

"So it's serious?"

"Totally," he said, matter-of-factly. "I'm still thinking about how amazing she looked last night. Been thinking about her all day. We went to this movie premiere and the paparazzi told me to get out of the way. Then they snapped like a million pictures of her."

"An actress?"

"No, she's a hairdresser. She does hair on movie sets. She's always super fashionable but last night she was over the top."

"What was she wearing?"

"High-waisted jeans, red suspenders, a tank top, and red heels. I swear! I'm going to marry this girl. She's so hot." He took out his phone and showed me a picture of her. I had to act as I did when friends showed me pictures of their newborn babies.

"She's *gor-geous*," I gulped, while he sat and flicked through her pictures.

This was what I liked and didn't like about Los Angeles. The vanity. Most of the people who lived here placed the highest importance on appearance. What did Warhol say? "I love Hollywood. They're beautiful. Everybody's plastic, but I love plastic. I want to be plastic." In Los Angeles, it was as if no one had heard about the impermanence of beauty, or the importance of intellectual chemistry. I wanted to tell Oscar what mattered most was the connection between two people, but I knew those connections changed, went haywire, so I refrained. To hell with depth. Maybe Oscar was onto something. Attraction was important, magnetic, and unavoidable. It could fade as fast as sidewalk chalk in a downpour, but while it lasted, what an explosive thing it was. This whole town thrived on youth and beauty.

"I'm not a bad looking guy," he said.

"You're holding your own."

"She's just too pretty for me," he replied, sounding less intelligent every second.

"I'm sure she feels the same way about you. How old are you anyway?"

"25." That made more sense, I thought. I got married at 25. I couldn't even remember 25. I envisioned the picture on my mantle: our arms around each other, and we're waving good-bye to our guests. Our freedom. We looked like kids. We were kids. Stupid, like this kid.

"I'm just afraid she'll break my heart."

Mae came back to the table and we talked about traffic until Oscar's girlfriend entered the bar, wearing a killer black dress, pointy heels, and a faux fur coat. Everyone in the bar kept their eyes on her. He immediately stood up, gave her a hug that started at her hips and moved upward to her chest, and pressed his fingers into the small of her back. His arms were all over her as they walked toward the DJ.

I suddenly felt exhausted. I could tell Mae had taken something, because she wouldn't stop talking and kept licking her lips, which was her tell. If I had to sit here any longer, I needed to talk about something more substantial.

"Cheever's journals," I interjected. "Have you read them?"

"No," she said. "I didn't even know he kept a journal."

"Exactly! Most people don't. They're so sad. "

"No one can end a story like him," Mae said.

"That's true," I responded. " Like when he ends that story with the guy hitting his brother in the head with a rock."

"It didn't end there," Mae replied. "It ends when his wife and sister come out of the sea naked." She looked deep within herself, then said Cheever's exact words, "Unshy and graceful."

I leaned back in my chair and marveled at her ability to recite literature. No one had that skill anymore. "Say it again."

"Unshy and graceful."

"Yes! That's it—exactly," I said, and the vision of the two naked women coming out of the water blurred with Mae sitting in the candle-light.

"I like the story about the middle-age guy who jumps over the furniture," Mae said. "I remember reading that story in high school and thinking that guy was so old, but he's probably our age now. It's one of his Shady Hill suburb bits."

"I just read that story again!" I said, thinking it couldn't be a coincidence. There were no coincidences. This conversation was supposed to happen. Mae and I, as ridiculous as we were, had conversations that mattered. "When his wife goes over to her friend's house and cries about the meaning of marriage and the meaning of love? And how they don't necessarily match. It's still relevant. The friend tells her that she should get a job and have financial and emotional freedom…"

"You know what I think about that." Mae looked at me quizzically, or was she just high?

"Are you talking about me?" My voice was suddenly high-pitched.

"You don't have a job or financial freedom."

"I work," I said, trembling.

Her eyebrows raised in a challenge.

"What I do is a hell of a lot harder than what you do and you know it!"

"I'm not saying it's not," she said, "but don't you want to have something of your own?"

"Of course I do," I yelled over the music, "but you can't have both!"

Mae prematurely crushed her cigarette as if she was going to storm off to the bathroom and do some more drugs, because didn't she have both? Who would she be if she didn't have both? Of course she had both. It was all over her Instagram. Her fashion blog. It was now my turn to raise my eyebrow at her, but she just looked at me pathetically.

"I just couldn't leave my babies with a stranger," I said.

"But they're all in school now."

"And they all get out at different times. I have to drive them to soccer, basketball, volley ball. Get groceries. Go to theater arts. Guitar lessons and shit."

"You can pay a college student to do that!"

"Who is going to hire me now?" I yelled. "I haven't had a job for over a decade. What could I do that would be more important than the job I have? Be a copywriter for Pottery Barn for Christ's sake?"

Mae laughed.

Then I laughed.

"What about your short stories?" She took out a new cigarette.

"What about them? They're still there. People aren't banging on my door to publish them."

"Don't you have to send things to publishers in order to get published?"

"I can't do it right now," I said. "You know what one definition of stress is, being in one place and wanting to be in another. I had to give something up. So presently, I'm the nanny. And I'm trying to be grateful for every minute because pretty soon they're going to be gone, and I want to have a good relationship with them."

Mae winced, as if I said that she wasn't going to have a good relationship with her son, which wasn't what I meant. "Maybe my stories aren't any good? Maybe it's no big loss." I lit a cigarette and looked at my friend, "If only I had your nanny's salary."

"You'd be killing it," she replied.

Just then, a guy with a flat-billed Dodgers hat stood over the table. "Can I take this chair?"

"No," Mae said. "We're waiting for a friend."

I remembered the thousand dollars. I didn't know how much longer I could sit here. I wanted to cry and take off my heels. After my drink, I asked her if we could go back to the hotel, and to my surprise, she said yes. We linked arms and leaned into each other as we walked up the cobblestone driveway. We said goodnight to the valet guys, like we'd known them for years. In front of us was Neil.

"Neil!" I screamed, drunk.

Mae, high and composed, just smiled.

"Ladies!" He hugged us.

I grabbed his arm for assistance. I could feel his large muscles under his cashmere.

"You like touching my arms, don't you?" he asked in an avuncular tone that alarmed me. I almost retorted, *Muscles are so Venice Beach*. But I caught myself and said, "I haven't felt muscles in a while. Maybe a lifetime."

"Would you two like to come up to my bungalow for a drink?" he asked.

"I've always wanted to see the bungalows," Mae replied.

"I could have another drink," I said.

Neil's meticulous room was a couple floors above ours and had a balcony overlooking Sunset Boulevard. We sat on the couch in the living room that opened up to his bedroom. He offered us some champagne. Mae took out a tiny package and asked Neil if he wanted some. His face became tense, and I answered for him, "I don't think Neil has ever done a drug in his life."

"I haven't," his eyes shifted. "But I'm not opposed to you doing them."

"She fancies herself a psychic," Mae said to Neil.

"It was just a guess," I replied, looking at his spotless room.

Mae twirled her thick hair into a bun. She sat with her bare legs on the red embroidered rug. She offered me a line, but I shook my head. It was past midnight, and I wanted to sleep. She shrugged her shoulders and emptied the package on the glass table. Mae did drugs elegantly like it was the 1970s, without shame or consequences.

"When I saw you guys outside," Neil said. "I thought you were a couple."

"That isn't the first time someone has thought that," Mae replied.

"You'd make a beautiful couple," Neil said.

"We love each other," Mae said, looking at me. "We've been

friends for a long time."

"If you were a couple, which one of you would be the guy?" Neil asked, not caring about our friendship at all.

I snarled at Mae. This conversation felt as outdated as Neil's muscles. Of course he didn't mind if we did drugs. Get as high as you want, honey, then I will suggest the predictable threesome. I got up to get a glass of water. Then Neil said to me, "You are most certainly the girl."

"I can't believe you just said that," Mae said, upset. "Why is she the girl?"

"A woman," I yelled from the kitchen. "I'm officially a woman." I located a glass and filled it with tap water. "He's generalizing on physical appearance. You're 5'11. I'm 5'8."

"Mae clearly knows what she wants," Neil replied. "She's in control."

"And being indecisive is a female trait?"

"Being in control is masculine," he replied.

When I returned from the kitchen, Mae was sitting closer to Neil. There was a new intimacy between them that I didn't understand nor want to be a part of. "No, he's right," Mae said. "My voice is hoarse. I'm bigger. I am more dominant."

I looked at Mae in disbelief. She suddenly created this narrative where she was this big bossy thing that no one had ever loved, and Neil was right there to comfort her.

"Mae," Neil sat on the edge of the couch and touched her thigh, like he was going to set her straight, take away all her past insecurities, and give her newfound confidence, "you're intimidatingly beautiful."

I rolled my eyes, watching Mae drink in the male attention. She untied her hair, it fell around her shoulders covering half of her face, and then pushed it behind her ear. I wondered if the need to be desired was a female or male trait? Regardless, Mae was hungry for it.

"I'm not afraid to ask for what I want," she paused. "Men don't look at me like a girl they can save."

"Have you read Cheever, Neil?" I interjected.

"What?" Neil was under some spell.

"We were talking about John Cheever earlier. I'm reading his journals right now."

"Sure," he answered.

"She's very feminine," Mae said, pointing at me. "And flirty. Everyone always falls in love with Emma because she's nurturing."

"I'm the least nurturing person I know."

"She's very open," Neil said to Mae.

"Yeah, I'm open to meeting people. Having shenanigans. But that's about as open as I get, Neil."

"It's how she gets through her mundane life," Mae said to Neil.

"Everyone's life is mundane!" I snapped at Mae. Then looked at Neil, "She doesn't understand that some people can find pleasure staying home with their children."

"She got married too young. That's why she's out all the time," Mae said. "She's a late bloomer. She's still looking for something."

"Isn't everyone looking for something?" I retorted. "Can you name one person who is satisfied with their life? Seriously, aren't we all anticipating some kind of salvation? Or escaping in one way or another? My life is not less than yours, because I don't have a career. And yeah, you're killing it right now, but you're on the verge of a nervous breakdown. You take three horse pills of Adderall each day, and you wonder why your adrenal glands are shot. Or why your kid would rather be with his nanny."

They both nodded their heads at me like it was good that I got this out. That they were proud of me for telling them my true feelings. Which I didn't even think were true. I was just exhausted and annoyed.

"Have you ever been dominated?" Neil asked me, and Mae remained perfectly calm, like it was the most sensible question anyone had ever asked.

"What do you think?" Mae asked, like she'd spent a lifetime in a dungeon.

The room suddenly felt cold. Sterile. It felt like I'd been set up. Was Neil the professional and Mae made me believe that I was the one who wanted to come up here? I carefully placed my feet back in my shoes.

"It's late," I said.

"You're not going anywhere," Mae snapped. "It's not even two and we don't have to wake up tomorrow." She turns to Neil, "She's not used to me getting more attention than her."

"That's not true." I stood up.

"Sit down," Neil said calmly. Then he walked over to his dresser and opened the bottom drawer. He pulled out a long black whip. Mae sat up straight, her eyes fascinated with the whip. I started looking for a phone just in case I needed to call the front desk.

"It's called a cat of nine tails. Do you want to touch it?"

"No," I said. "I'm good."

Mae stroked the whip. "It's so soft," she said.

"It reminds me of Mary Gaitskill's *Secretary*," I said. "Have you read the short story?"

"Only seen the movie," Neil responded, passing Mae the whip.

"She's a writer," Mae said, gripping the handle.

"I'm a mother," I replied. "We're *both* mothers."

Neil did not flinch. He was old enough to have had experiences with women who also happened to be mothers. Neil took the handle from Mae's hand and held it while she petted the tails. She placed one of the tails in my hand. The three of us sat there connected by the whip.

HOLY COMMUNION

y seven-year-old lies on the fuzzy rug in her shared bedroom. The ball of her right foot rests on her left, and her arms stretch out in a T. Her eyes flutter as she drops her right ear to her shoulder.

"What are you doing?" I ask, carrying in a basket of folded laundry.

"Playing Jesus dying on the cross," Chloe answers for her older sister. "He has nails in his boobies!"

I roll my eyes and tickle little Jesus' feet. Grace kicks with laughter then grows gravely serious. "Jesus died, Mommy. He really did."

"He has nails in his boobies." Chloe lifts up her polka dot top.

"Noo-oh!" Grace insists. "The nails are in his feet and in his wrists and he has thorns sticking into his head and blood trickles down his body. He's slumped over like this." She strikes her pose.

"Okay, honey." I pause, looking past my tired reflection, past our garden, beyond the wooden fence and into our neighbor's kitchen. I'm trying to think of the right thing to say. I want to tell her she's too young to hear these stories, to have these images injected into her head. Her Holy Communion book is open and I'm supposed to read it with her. I read the first paragraph to myself for "Station 4: Jesus Meets His Mother":

Jesus, you feel so alone with all those people yelling and screaming at you. You don't like the words they are saying about you, and you look for a friendly face in the crowd. You see your mother. She can't make the hurting stop, but

*it helps to see that she is on your side, that she is suffering
with you. She does understand and care.*

"MA-mee. MA-mee. MA-mee!" One of them is chanting. Maybe both. I close the book and wonder if my fears of having my children grow up differently than me is causing them harm. As a child, Catholicism gave me both comfort and fear. I remember sympathizing with Mary's predicament so much that I convinced myself I could be the second Immaculate Conception. Even though I spent my twenties undoing most of my programmed beliefs, the scriptures were still ingrained in my thinking. I couldn't comprehend raising fundamentally good humans without the Ten Commandments.

"Enough Jesus talk for today," is all I can muster. "It's time for bed."

Chloe jumps into her twin bed and Grace reluctantly walks over to hers. Over the guardrail, I kiss Chloe on her freckled nose. "Put on the magic," she demands. I stir two imaginary pots then wave my fingers over her from head to toe. I mumble fake spells with the power of a sorceress. "Good night, Lo," I whisper. She's practically asleep by the time I walk over to Grace's bed.

"Is the bread really his body?" Grace asks.

"I guess," I shrug. "It's more like a symbol."

"Is the wine really blood?"

"Not really."

"Can you read me something else?" She widens her blue eyes and her chest heaves. She's about to cry. Every night before bed, she looks like this.

"Not tonight, honey. Your brother still has one feeding in the middle of the night. I need to sleep. Let me put on the magic."

My hands wave with power. I utter gibberish. I believe the gibberish. I may be Emma the Sorceress, but I'm actually praying to Jesus that she falls asleep. Nothing works. The girl hates sleep. There are not enough books in the world for her to read. There are bad dreams even before she closes her eyes.

"Snuggle me," she begs.

I climb over her guardrail, the little white picket fence, and breathe into the curve of her warm neck. She hangs on me like a tire swing. We are in a meadow. There is a breeze and her swing is tied to my weeping willow. Her toes skim the pond. We no longer hear traffic. We no longer need alarms to alert us that someone has broken in. We don't care. Take the unpolished silver, the obligatory china, the Waterford Crystal. Earthquake, come now. We sleep intertwined like branches.

The grinding of her teeth wakes me: marbles crushed by an elephant's foot. By the sound of it, she will wake up with jagged teepees in her small mouth, a mound of gravel cutting her pink gums. I don't know if I should wake her. Is the bone crushing sound disturbing me or is she actually breaking her teeth? I attempt to massage the hinge of her jaw, but her eyelids tighten and she shakes me off with her hand.

Leave her alone. I climb over the guardrail, walk down the hall and get in my own bed. I write a note to call the dentist. I pray to God, The Universe, Buddha, my grandmother and my Great Aunt Patty. Never to Mary. Never to my grandfather.

I ask them: Why am I passing on this religion? Why does a seven-year-old grind her teeth? What is she afraid of? Please, I say, just for one night...take away the things that scare her. *Give them to me.*

I've had this dream so many times that I tell myself, *This Is The Dream*. My skin is sewed to my duvet cover with a black thread. It is the exact spool that had stitched my lips back together when the neighbor's dog ripped my face in two at age seven. I remember looking in the mirror at my unzipped face, both sides of my lips blown to my ears. My gums and bones, exposed like a skeleton. It's Thanksgiving so the doctor who is stitching me up is an intern. My mom holds me down, her neck craned away. I know she hurts as much as I do; yet, there is nothing she can do. Does it help to see that she is on my side, suffering with me? Or does realizing that she can't protect me make it worse?

I'm somewhere between asleep and awake and my body is immobilized. *Wake up*. I'm stronger than this thread that has sewn my face back together, but it is taut like fishing wire. When I try to sit up, something pulls it tighter. I'm startled by the sound of running feet. My eyelids are glued shut but I feel the girls jumping on my paralyzed body, my full bladder. Their heels dig into my quadriceps. They step on my shins. My head whips back and forth in pain, but I don't want to frighten them.

"Mommy, where are you?" Grace shouts.

"Get the scissors," I say calmly in my other voice. "Cut the black thread." But they don't hear me.

"Mommy!" she screams.

My formless self rises from my body and I tiptoe away from the girls like a ghost. But I'm not a ghost. I'm a seven-year-old-girl who sees crucified monsters. They jump off my body on the bed, their feet pounding on the floor, climbing the stairs. I hear them getting closer, then I feel them shake me awake. I look at their bright faces and my eyes fill with tears.

"Why are you up here?" Chloe asks, gleefully. "Did you sleep upstairs?"

"I don't know," I reply. "I must've been sleepwalking. I had a bad dream." I'm sitting on the playroom floor next to a plastic toy kitchen. I push my hair out of my face, extend my arms, and pull them into the willow tree. They watch the sap pour from my eyes. They don't know that mommies can cry yet. They are mystified.

"Are you crying?" Chloe asks. "Mommy's crying!" she says to her older sister. "Why is mommy crying?"

I let the tears fall down my face and Chloe catches them purposefully with her finger.

"I know why you are crying," Grace looks at me closely. "You're crying because you are happy," she says confidently. "You're crying because the world is so beautiful."

SATURDAY MOURNING

Just before sunrise, Tanya and her older sister Nicole drove to a clinic three suburbs away in one of the wealthy neighborhoods they rarely visited. Neither of the girls spoke in the car, nor turned on the radio. Tanya noticed more trees in this town and that there weren't any sidewalks, just big houses spread far apart from each other, very different from their apartment complex and the surrounding, glued-together buildings. The elm trees in this part of Illinois concealed the clinic so much they almost missed their turn.

When they pulled into the parking lot, they saw a family of geese walking across the narrow path that led to the rust-colored building with two middle-aged women and one man standing out in front. Their eyes were closed, their hands folded beneath girthy bellies, and their lips mumbled unsynchronized prayers.

"Don't look when we walk past them." Nicole stared into her sister's eyes that were the same color brown as hers, except Tanya *had* flecks of amber around her pupils.

Tanya nodded.

Nicole cut the ignition and before Tanya's hand reached the door, white knuckles knocked on the glass. Tanya flinched then looked up to find a thin woman with an angular face, watery blue eyes, and shiny coral lips. The lady motioned for Tanya to roll down the window. Tanya looked at Nicole who gestured to her to get out of the car. Cautiously, Tanya opened the door.

"Good morning," the woman said kindly.

"Hey," Tanya replied. Her eyes moved up and down the lady's velour sweat suit. Tanya had a jumpsuit just like that at home, but the lady's fabric looked more plush, less faded, a velvety midnight blue. The lady's hair, still wet from her morning shower, was slicked back into a low bun; her white skin was dewy.

"Are you with the clinic?" Nicole spoke over the roof of their red Civic.

The lady smiled calmly at Nicole then lowered her voice and spoke only to Tanya, "Has anyone talked to you about your options?"

"Options?" Tanya repeated.

"You must feel different," the lady replied.

Tanya gazed at the wide spreading roots of an old elm tree. She had felt something take space in her body almost immediately. She didn't even have to wait for the Plus sign or the day after her missed period. She just knew. There was no doctor's appointment or ultrasound taken. She'd only told her boyfriend, then Nicole, who said she'd take care of it.

"Do you know how far along you are?" the lady asked.

Tanya kept her eyes on the elm's slippery bark. Thanks to the Internet, she knew everything. She knew it was the size of a kidney bean, and if she waited any longer—a blueberry—then, a kumquat. She'd never tasted a kumquat, and now she never would, because it was a fruit that she wanted to forget. She nodded yes.

"What's your name?" the lady asked softly.

Tanya knew not to say her name.

"I'm Laura. And I'm here to help you."

Nicole shut the door and walked over. "You with the clinic?"

Laura held Tanya's gaze. "Do you want to talk to someone before you go in there?"

"If not," Nicole said, "I suggest you leave us alone."

Tanya's bare legs melted into the blacktop. Swarms of hidden insects hummed in the green foliage that covered them like a tent. The buzzing of the cicadas intensified to a high-pitch screech, then lulled to a hushed vibration. In the distance, she saw the family of geese pecking at the grass.

"Please get out of her way." Nicole placed her hand on Tanya's arm.

"I'm not in her way," Laura said, never taking her eyes off Tanya. "I'm here to support you."

Nicole looked confused. "What can *you* do?"

"I'm giving her a voice," Laura looked at Nicole for the first time.

Nicole stood taller than both of them with broad shoulders and a long neck. She wore a gray tank top and purple mesh shorts. Her carved legs made Laura think that she ran track. Laura envisioned hurdles, batons, the triple jump...anything she could to find a way to connect with her. In high school, Laura ran the 800 and 1,600 relays. She still ran about three miles a day. If only she could make them understand that nine months was such a short period of time and if Tanya wanted to play sports like her older sister, she could. Laura had two children in her thirties and she still ran a mile at the same pace she had when she was eighteen. The age she guessed Tanya was now.

"Have you talked to anyone about this?" Laura asked Tanya.

Tanya's eyes moved from the roots of the tree to its patient trunk and fanning branches. The only other person she'd indirectly discussed this with was her AP Physics teacher, Mr. Plett. She'd approached him because he was the only non-Catholic person that she knew and she respected the way he viewed the world. When Mr. Plett spoke in class his eyes looked past her and the other students into the cosmos as if he knew some truth that they didn't. He went on about sound waves, static electricity, and all the other types of energy. Real things that were all around us that we couldn't see.

The day after she knew Nicole made the appointment, she waited after the bell rant to speak with Mr. Plett. She listened to chairs slamming into desks and shoes pivoting on the floor, they were the same sounds she heard when she asked him for a letter of recommendation and when she showed him her acceptance letter from the University of Illinois.

"Whatcha dreaming up now?" Mr. Plett opened a container of Lemon Clorox wipes.

"Just thinking about what Einstein said about energy. That it couldn't be destroyed."

"Only changed from one form to another." Mr. Plett finished her sentence.

"And you believe him?" Tanya felt hopeful.

"I do."

"But what about things like...I don't know...if something ceases to exist, can it come back again at a different time? Like, when you were ready?"

"Is there something specific that you need to talk about?"

"No. You just got me thinking, that's all."

She gave him a distant smile and turned on her shoe.

"Tanya Marie, walk around her," Nicole said.

"I have an idea," Laura spoke to them both. "Why don't you come across the street with me to the Birth Choice Health Clinic and talk to a counselor, and if you still decide to come back over here, I will walk you in, myself. The counselors have all the resources you need."

"Resources?" Nicole raised her tone.

"There are tons of resources available to you if you walk next door."

Tanya looked over at the clumpy soil. Her body pulsed with the insects. She'd just learned about natural resources. She pictured waterfalls, windmills, and creeks. She wondered what this woman could do for her?

"Who do you think you are?" Nicole shook her head at Laura. "Messing with people's lives."

"I help people get information and support," Laura retorted. Her voice sounded a little robotic, like it came from a script in a three-ring binder. She reminded herself to stay calm. To make it personal. "I'm here for Tanya."

Nicole tapped her foot on the pavement. Hearing this woman say her sister's name enraged her. The woman used it like a weapon and Nicole had handed it to her. This woman didn't care about Tanya, she didn't even know Tanya, the girl with the wizard brain. That's what mom called her and it was true. Nicole could barely keep up in school, used her legs to get a volleyball scholarship to Rockford University. Tanya would be the second person in their entire family to ever go to college. The first on an academic scholarship. This woman didn't know how hard she had to work to receive an education. The only thing this lady cared about was her own beliefs. Nicole held her anger back. To protect Tanya from this, she'd driven to the clinic yesterday to make sure there weren't any picketers or zealots jumping out of bushes screaming verses from Deuteronomy. The praying people were there, but they didn't even look at her as she sailed past them to confirm her appointment. The gold Lexus with the *God's Pro-Life* bumper sticker was nowhere to be found.

Now Nicole wanted to peel it off, and if her nails had been longer, she would have. Instead, Nicole walked around Laura's Gold SUV and looked in the passenger window. There were two cow-print car seats the size of thrones, multiple pairs of designer sunglasses, and a mountain of headbands on the dashboard. Spools of ribbon, fabric gerbera daisies, and plastic jewels sparkled in the passenger seat. It looked like Christmas, but it was July.

"I want to go to college," Tanya finally spoke to no one in particular. "You don't understand."

That was what Laura heard the most. Everyone thought that she couldn't possibly understand. That termination was the only way. She wanted to tell Tanya about the Muslim family that she'd helped. The family found out by ultrasound that their third child would be born with a cleft palate and a tumor on its brain. Using her resources, Laura told the couple how cleft palates were surgically fixed, and how most tumors dissolved in utero. Laura mentioned that her sister was a doctor and could help them find a specialist. She even offered to watch their two older children while they went to that specialist. In the end, she didn't do any of those things, but it was the offering that made the couple stop and think. Laura knew once people walked across the street, it was highly unlikely that they would return to the clinic.

Laura saw the couple walk away holding hands, but she wondered if they came back another day or if they drove to another town. She was only able to make it on Saturdays when her husband stayed with the girls. Maybe because that couple had two daughters around the same age as her own, she thought of them often. She prayed daily that the tumor would dissolve, that their insurance would cover all of the surgeries, and that they made the right decision. She wanted to follow up immediately, but because she wasn't a certified counselor yet, she didn't have access to their files.

One day when no one was around, Laura took it upon herself to find the couple's information. She left two messages until she finally got a hold of the mother.

"Hi. I'm Laura from the health clinic. Do you remember me?"

"Yes," the woman paused. "I do."

With some coercing from Laura, the woman explained that they'd given birth to another baby girl and after the hardest year of their life, their daughter's face had healed. When Laura asked about the tumor, the woman said that it was benign. Laura felt overjoyed for the mother. A true miracle! All her prayers had been answered. The woman never thanked Laura. She actually hung up on her, but Laura knew what would have happened if she wasn't sitting in the parking lot that Saturday morning.

"I've helped others," Laura said to Tanya, "I can help you, too."

Because of the conviction in her voice, Tanya almost believed her. In some ways, she was helping her now, slowing down the process, and loosening the knots in her stomach. She didn't know exactly what this woman could do, but it felt like she could reverse time, stop the sperm from back-flipping into her ovaries, and release the air out of her swelling breasts.

"So what do you say?" Laura looked at Tanya, "Can I walk you over?"

Nicole let out a sigh. "Don't you think this is hard enough?"

Nicole wanted to grab Laura by her Juicy jumpsuit, lift her manicured toes off the asphalt, and spike her shiny face with her open palm. Instead, she took deep breaths through flared nostrils and crushed her with her eyes.

Tanya remained perfectly still. Tears dropped down her tight face. She didn't know what to do. She just wanted to go back to her old self. Nothing felt right. She tried to breathe, but her lungs were the size and weight of a change purse. Laura's watery eyes held her and, for a moment, Tanya felt like this woman could save her. She'd this strange feeling that Laura shared her sorrow, a loss that she could not express or forget. Tanya wanted to rest her cheek on her velvety shoulder and cry for both of their unhealed wounds. As Laura studied the designs around Tanya's pupils, she felt like she'd been seen for the first time. No one else had looked at her with such warmth.

Everyone only saw the silver lining: Laura's two blue-eyed, piano-playing, tap-dancing girls. They did not see the tiny feet. Smaller than a flightless bird's claws. Perfectly formed. When Laura's placenta detached from her uterus, causing her to hemorrhage, the doctors gave her an emergency C-section at only twenty weeks. She'd actually heard someone say, "It was only twenty weeks." Like it made a difference. Laura knew she already had two healthy daughters. That she should be grateful. But now, she was a woman without a womb who had held her dead baby in her arms. The experience deformed her. It felt like it was as obvious as talking without teeth. But no one knew. They only saw the outside. Which was, impossibly, unchanged.

When what was supposed to be her middle child, who would now always be her youngest, asked, "What happened to the baby?" she answered, "It decided not to come after all."

"Can we get a trampoline instead?"

For months Laura watched her girls do sit-and-stands, straddle kicks, and front somersaults, while she recalled those tiny feet. Instead of going to mass only on Sundays, she went everyday, then back to the couch. She bought a sewing machine, spools of ribbons: lime green and hot pink, light blue and brown, yellow and orange. Nantucket colors, she thought. She made a closet full of hair bows and sold them to the boutiques with names like Born Beautiful, Bugs and Kisses, and Chocolate Soup. Nothing helped. On a Tuesday, she saw the Volunteers Needed flier in the parish hall and finally, something did.

"Let's go learn about your baby," Laura said, and Tanya winced.

It was too early to say that word. If only she would've said kumquat.

"I want to go home," Tanya turned to Nicole, who walked to the driver's side of the Civic.

"I'll pray for you, Tanya," Laura said a little too loudly and Nicole paused.

"Tanya, get in the car." And when she slammed the door, Nicole shouted, "Go to hell," loud enough that the praying people opened their eyes, scary enough to frighten Laura back into her gold Lexus and lock the door.

Nicole peeled out of the parking lot with her hand on her sister's leg. Tanya pressed her hand on top of Nicole's while she looked at the smeared goose droppings that covered the path. They will go to another clinic downtown with screaming protestors hurling rotten fruit at her legs. Only the lady with the watery blue eyes will haunt them.

THE BEATING

I'm lying on the operating table crucifix-style with leather straps binding my arms. The needle in my spine has erased my body. I am only a head.

"You won't be able to feel your lungs," my doctor says, "but you're still breathing."

Just then, something holds my breath. It feels like I'm underwater. I wonder how long I can hold this, like swimming the length of a pool, there and back. I want to blindly touch the wall, but there is no coming up. I'm suffocating. The beeping intensifies. An alarm goes off. My eyes flicker into the fluorescent lights.

"Is she okay?" my husband asks.

"Her vitals are fine," my doctor replies.

I turn my head away from them and clench my face. I wonder if my body is sobbing, if my heart is beating.

"Can we untie one of her hands?" my doula begs. "So she can at least feel her breath?"

"I guess," the doctor says.

Someone unbuckles my right hand. I watch my fingers wiggle. I cover my mouth and miraculously, I feel the tiniest *hah* on my palm. I'm breathing like I'm fogging up a mirror. Suddenly, my temperature drops. A freezing sensation envelops me as if they are putting me on ice. I hear a knocking sound that is louder than the beeping and buzzing. I listen to it as I *hah*, *hah*, *hah* into my hand.

"Is there anything you can do about her shaking?" my husband asks.

"The shaking is normal," the doctor says.

I look at my husband, who is wearing scrubs but not a mask, and he looks incredibly young, too young to see his wife trembling on a table.

"Can we put a blanket under her elbow?" my doula suggests. "Her elbow is banging the table."

The doctor's face behind her mask is unfazed by the sound. She sighs. A nurse appears. Two folded blankets are placed under my arm. The beating stops, and strangely, I miss it. It was the only organic sound in the room.

"Emma, I'm going to make the incision now," the doctor says.

She cuts through my tissues, slowly carving her way to my uterus. When she reaches my abdominal muscles, she separates them with her hands like my mother, who is waiting outside, used to unbraid my hair.

"We have the baby's feet," says the doctor. "You're going to feel some pressure."

I am so grateful to feel anything that I almost say, "Hurt me." The doctor's hands knead my stomach like dough. She rises on her toes as she flattens me out. I can only feel the pressure. When the pressing stops, the pulling begins. Deadlock. The doctor versus the body that I'm harboring inside me. Its stubborn head stuck underneath my right rib. Its unwillingness to turn is why I'm being cut open. I don't know how I know this or even if it's true, but I know the doctor's hands are around the baby's ankles and I can feel her tugging life out of my incision. The doctor takes one step back and pulls out something the size of the universe.

AAAAH, I breathe into my hand.

The doctor lifts up this white mass of pulsing flesh, high above the blue sheet like a sacrifice, and asks my husband, not me, "Do you want to announce the sex?"

No one responds.

She repeats herself. She holds the baby that is not bloody but covered in toothpaste under the bright lights. Its white face tightens but doesn't make a sound.

"It's...it's a...?" She angles its swollen genitals to my husband.

"Girl?" he says, and the doctor nods, yes. Color rushes to my husband's face. I only thought it was an expression, but he looks like he might actually jump with joy. I close my eyes. I know somewhere I am deeply happy, but I cannot feel exhilaration—yet. My heart is cold. Even colder than the ice bath my girlhood is drowning in. Tears fall from my eyes.

"Why is she white?" I ask in the thinnest voice. "Is she okay? She hasn't cried. She isn't moving."

"It's called vernix," the doctor replies. "Babies that are early are still covered in it."

Somebody wraps her up. They hold her white goo to my face. I turn my neck. She has huge purple lips. My husband's lips. They hand her to him. His entire being blazes into her barely-opened eyes. The genetic blueprint passes, and it's instant love for them. I perform a smile and watch my husband, whose abdomen is still intact, bleed with happiness, while I bleed somewhere behind the blue sheet. And instead of being moved, I think: *I transformed, while you, you only watched.*

A team of eager scrubs come in and take her to a plastic case. Somebody tells me that they are checking her vitals. Her vitals are good. My husband follows them. Leaves me. Rolls the baby outside to my mother. My mother is waving and holding the baby. She will still be holding the baby when I'm rolled into post-op to wait for my body to unthaw. But for now, I'm left with the women—the doula, two doctors, and a nurse.

"That was 13 minutes," my doctor says. "We have about 30 more."

I remove my hand from my mouth and sink to the bottom. I watch my doctor as if she is working on someone else. Her movements are small and her eyes are intense but not unkind. She tells me she is removing my placenta. I hear something wet splash into a bucket. She rearranges my organs, cupping them with her hands, and glues me back together. The doula begins rubbing my scalp, pulling me out by my hair.

I am closed up.

My husband walks beside me as they wheel my bed into another room. My nose itches from the morphine the nurse has injected, but I can't scratch yet. I still can't lift my arms or wiggle my toes. I see my mother rocking the baby, who is wrapped in a footprint blanket. Someone has placed a tiny pink-and-blue-striped cap on her hairless head. I look down at my limbs as if the heat of my stare will melt the anesthesia away. It doesn't. Someone could stick a knitting needle through my thigh and I wouldn't even know.

My doctor swoops in. She lifts up my gown, removes the maxi pad that one of the nurses had placed on top of my wound to absorb my blood, and smiles at my incision. She's pleased with her work.

"She's the best," the nurse says. "You'll hardly scar."

I narrow my eyes at the nurse and look at my doctor, who, two years from now, will remove her mask and kiss my cheek after she delivers my second daughter, vaginally. Two years after that, she will save my son, who will be born with the umbilical cord so tightly wrapped around his neck that his face will be blue and bruised like a boxer. But at this moment, she asks, "Would you like to have him circumcised?"

I look at her so intensely that she catches her mistake. "I'm sorry," she says, "that was my fourth C-section today." She places my folder in the pocket on the door and walks away down the hall.

A lifetime later, my lungs start to take shape. I flutter-kick my feet. Roll my ankles. Bend my knees. I flip my palms to the ceiling and make a fist. I bring my hands to my shoulders like I'm lifting an imaginary barbell. I open my jaw, one last hah.

"I'm ready," I say to my mom and my husband.

My mother hands me Grace, and I look at my daughter as if it's the first time.

A DIGNIFIED MAN

I had one week left of my 90-day sentence in the county jail, for my second DWI, when Maria told me about my stepfather's cancer. We spoke on black phones, separated by a plastic wall. I wore a red jumpsuit, and Maria, a brightly patterned sundress.

"I don't get it," I said. "The doctors just told him he was in remission."

"Your mom thought it was a routine procedure but when they opened him up, it was everywhere. They gave him six weeks. I feel so bad for her. First your dad, now George." She sat up straight and placed her fist by her face like a tiny boxer. "But she's being very brave."

The guard was eavesdropping and looking at Maria. I stared at him until he looked away.

"Is anyone bothering you?" Maria asked, and I wondered if I looked like something *had* happened, or if I looked like the same clean-cut guy that she'd met waiting tables at the Odd Duck. I wondered why 19-year-old Maria was there at all.

"No one's bothering me," I replied untruthfully. "I'll be home in less than a week."

"Time's up." One of the guards walked over.

"I love you," she said.

I put my hand on the glass.

"Jonathan," George murmured, waking me out of a daze. "The kettle is hissing."

I walked into the kitchen and poured hot water into the oatmeal, sliced the bananas, and poured some apple juice. I placed the television tray in front of his chair, knowing he would only eat a spoonful or two. "Just how you like it, warm with cold bananas."

"Thank you." He coughed and spat red mucus into a silver bucket.

As if lying down equaled death, George dwelt in the La-Z-Boy chair next to the hospital bed in our living room. The sun forced its way through half-open shutters, and George asked if I could do something about the light. I walked over and made sure that each panel slanted in the same direction, making the three windows perfectly symmetrical. Then I sat down on the couch. George kept looking at me, or looking beyond me, so I asked, "Do you need to go to the bathroom?" We'd bought a portable toilet and I would roll it into the living room and lift George from one chair to the other. But he just shook his head. The colon cancer had taken all the color out of his face. His skin was a grayish tone and it flaked when touched. Around two o'clock he said, "I'm sorry that I ruined your birthday."

"Don't worry about it," I replied. "It's not like I have any friends to celebrate with." I looked at the light coming out of the shutters and remembered Zack and I in our old apartment. He had both hands in his long hair, pulling at it with his fists. He couldn't believe he'd lost the rent envelope. I helped him search every room. We lifted the mattress and ripped the cushions off the couch. I still remember my fake disappointment when all I found was potato chips, dust bunnies, and a penny. The entire time the envelope pressed against my hip.

I shook my head and looked straight into George's cloudy eyes and said, "There's no place I'd rather be."

The sincerity in my voice startled me. Since I'd been taking care of George, I'd started daydreaming about going to nursing school, working in a hospital, being in dark blue scrubs surrounded by a sea of salmon-colored scrubs. They'd call me in for the most physically demanding and disturbing cleanups because nothing bothered me. I knew the truth. The body could be barbaric and undignified with its uncontrolled fluids and odors, but I could see past it. I could separate the failing body from the dignified man. I still looked at George as the guy whe'd worked for the same company since he was 18. They didn't make guys like him anymore. I wished there was another name for a male nurse, something more masculine.

The garage door squealed open and George muttered, "You need to put some oil on that."

"Yes, sir," I said, as my mom walked in with a bag full of groceries.

"There's more in the trunk." She shot me a smile, lines shaped like wings curled around the corners of her eyes, and I couldn't help thinking that they looked good on her.

"I'll get up." I stood from my chair.

"I know you will," she smiled. My mother had adopted a southern accent after living in Texas for 20 years. "You warm enough, George?" she asked. "It's freezing in here. Jon, will you turn the AC down? And bring in the cake. It's on the front seat."

"Yes, ma'am," I replied as I closed the door behind me.

Except for the cake, my 30th birthday passed like every other night, with George in a half-sleep and my mom and me smoking cigarettes on the back porch, Maria quietly beside me. We reclined on white lawn chairs overlooking the pool and talked about the unruly grass that spring brought too quickly. The 80-degree heat melted the cake and caused sweat to run down the back of my legs. Maria's chest and collarbone glistened.

"I'll tackle the lawn on Sunday," I promised, squinting my eyes at the acre of grass.

"You looked just like your dad when you said that." My mom laughed and sipped her iced Chardonnay. "It's the eyes."

"I know, mom, an azure blue."

"The color of the sky on a clear summer's day," she said to Maria, who smiled politely.

"We got it, mom." I grabbed my pack of Camels and lit one. Then I flashed her a tight-lipped smile and passed her the cigarettes. My mom took her time striking the match, then she said to Maria, "You know I started smoking because I would have to go with Jon's dad to his teaching events. I didn't know a soul. Being an elementary school teacher, he was always surrounded by women, both teachers and parents. They were all educated and very well off. I never went to college and I didn't grow up with money so I always thought I stood out like a sore thumb. One evening, one of the fathers offered me a cigarette, and I smoked my brains out. It gave me something to do."

"Everyone in my family smokes," said Maria. "I never got into it."

My mom took a drag of her cigarette and replied, "His father remembered everyone's name. I couldn't remember those people if I met them 10 times. He was always a little better than me."

"Now that's not true," I interjected.

"Well, your grandmother thought so!"

"To hell with her," I smiled.

"That's right," my mom said. "We did alright without her, didn't we?"

Her dark eyes held mine and all I could think about was how

much I had disappointed her, all the nights when I was too drunk to call, all the mornings I'd found her sitting on the couch next to a mound of cigarette butts in a crystal ashtray. And, despite it all, we were still okay.

"She did go back to school," I told Maria. "When I went to UT, she got her AA. I'd call home and all my friends would be here studying with her."

"I remember you telling me that," Maria said.

"Jon always had a good group of friends." A smile split my mom's face, and the wings appeared, but shame caused my eyes to blink and I looked at the unlit pool.

"Happy birthday, son." She handed me a red box with a gift card from J.Crew and the movies. After my first stint in rehab and jail, no one trusted me with money. I stood up and gave her a kiss goodnight. Maria thanked her for dinner and the two of us went back to my childhood bedroom while my mom stayed outside, eyes glazed over, looking at the stars.

Maria sat on my bed painting her nails, while I drank whiskey from a silver flask that my ex Scarlett gave me before a college formal.

Maria said, "Do you ever think that you and your mom have a weird relationship?"

"All the time," I replied. "But we only have each other and we are only 20 years apart."

"It's like she doesn't even know that I'm here."

"That's not true. She likes you. If you feel so ignored," I teased, "why do you keep coming over?"

"I wonder," she said, looking at me. "Actually, I like staying here 'cause it's quiet," Maria continued. I shook my head, showing that I was listening, but from the moment I opened the flask and smelled the whiskey, Scarlett had slowly begun to enter the room. It used to be her in this bed. It used to be her smoking outside with my mom. The two of them, laughing like sisters. It felt strange doing the same things with a different person, but what are you supposed to do when someone rejects you? When someone that once loved you, no longer wants to see or hear from you again? The last time I saw Scarlett I was standing in the damp grass outside her window.

"Go away," she hissed. "You can't keep doing this."

"I just need to talk to you."

"There's nothing new to say. I can't keep going around in circles."

"Can you at least let me in and give me a goodbye hug?" I began whimpering.

"What good will it do? This is the only way I can help you. Now get out of here before I call the cops. You have to stop contacting me."

"What about all your stuff at my place? At least let me bring it over."

"Keep it," she said, shutting the window.

Maria's voice finally broke through my memory.

"My mom's always screaming at my brother, my dad at my mom, my mom at her aunt. You know, the one with the new baby, Angelica?"

I nodded blankly. I didn't remember the aunt, but I did remember the baby. Long eyelashes and pierced ears. She kept talking, so I sipped the flask and looked around my room. A fraternity paddle leaned against a bookshelf. On my dresser was a picture of my dad with his arm around me at age four. Signed baseballs were scattered around like Easter eggs. CDs and movies took up most of one wall, alphabetized and dust-free, each DVD a half-inch into the bookcase. A framed caricature of me drawn by Zack, who was now an artist in LA. A wave of pride and envy washed through me. I'd planned to go out there with him, but couldn't leave the state due to my first probation. Now it was too late to do something like that. Everyone else around me had been learning things, saving money, getting experience and moving out of Austin.

"I know this was a hard birthday for you," Maria said, blowing on her fingernails.

"For the longest time, I thought I'd never be older than my dad. That something bad would happen to me. Now that I am, it feels worse. Like I'm no longer praying to my dad, just some guy my age who probably knew less than I do now."

My eyes landed on the ball that Sparky Lyle signed. It was the last Rangers' game my dad had taken me to. We had seats right over the dugout and we used to wait for the players before and after the game. I wondered, as I often did, how different my life would've been had my father not gotten behind the wheel the night he died. I clung to the idea that his tragedy sealed my fate. I blamed his absence for my failures. I took one last sip, closed my eyes on all the could-have-beens, and buried myself in the covers. The whiskey made my body feel warm. I started drifting off to sleep, but Maria climbed on top of me, pulling me back to consciousness.

"Morning, George," I said, grabbing the bucket of red mucus.

"Morning, Jon." He looked alert.

"You remembered," I smiled. "Your parents are driving in from Ohio today."

"Sure did," he said. "My ma will tell me that I need to shave."

"Well, sir. A shave it is."

George put his arm around my neck and I carried him into the bathroom. I placed him on the toilet and spread shaving cream on his face. Then he said, "I can take it from here." I put my hands on his hollow back and helped him straighten up. It had been about a month since he'd seen himself. Each week he'd lost a significant amount of weight. His 135-pound frame no longer matched the person he knew. When he saw his sunken face and concave chest, he started to cry. I stood behind him, feeling his ribs shake in my hands. Out of respect, I looked down at the yellow shag rug that hugged the toilet. When he composed himself, I held him as he shaved an unrecognizable face.

His parents arrived an hour later. Betty and Bill Parker had driven an RV from Ohio to Texas. When I opened the door they were holding hands. They wore matching clothes: khaki pants with denim shirts. Betty needed a minute before she could walk in. She pressed her palms on her head to fix her windblown hair. Bill shook my hand and then extended his arm out to his wife and led her across the threshold.

"He's lost a lot of weight," I said, trying to prepare them for the sight of their son. They linked their arms together and walked slowly down the hallway. I could imagine them on their wedding day. Being small people, George's height must have surprised them. Now with his question mark spine and collapsing bones, he was their size. Betty and Bill's arms stayed linked as they huddled around their son. Watching them embrace, I had this notion that the love between parent and child transcended the body and was contained somewhere in a timeless vacuum. I felt the love my father had for me. Or was it the love I had for him? It was so powerful that I wanted it to go away. I needed a drink, and it was hours before my mom and George would be asleep and I could have one.

"Jonathan," George called, "come on out here and sit with us."

I sat down and looked at the black and white photos and listened to them talk about George as a child.

"He loved to ride his bike around town, he was never late for his paper route, and he called me—every Sunday—without ever missing a week," said Betty.

Hearing about George made me smile. The three of them really had something. I found myself questioning if George and I had missed an opportunity. It suddenly dawned on me that I could've loved him *and* been loyal to my dad. But, as always, I realized things too late. When the time came for Betty and Bill to leave, I gave them a moment alone with their son and then I walked them to the door. Betty hugged me tightly and said, "Make good choices, you hear?"

"I'll take care of him," I replied. The sincerity returned.

That evening, I downed George's bottle of codeine. He'd moved onto morphine, so I felt all right about swiping it. When Maria came over and climbed into bed with me, her long hair tickled my shoulders just like Scarlett's did and I got confused. I held onto Scarlett-Maria like a life preserver. My forehead nestled in the space between her shoulder blades. Maria must have felt my intensity because she started wiggling around. I must've said Scarlett's name because before I knew it, we were fighting and Maria was lying beside me crying. I put my arm around her, unable to open my eyes. Bright colors danced behind my lids: fuchsia, turquoise, and lime.

In my body, everything felt like it was smiling. Maria, so young and lovely, can't you see that I am poison? My skin sang to her, and she must've heard it because she stopped crying. As I melted into sleep, I felt Maria being pulled away by some forceful current.

In the morning, Maria was gone. I squirted liquid morphine into George's mouth with a syringe. Then I put on rubber gloves to spread a morphine gel on his arms and legs. He could no longer swallow pills. All this was supposed to make him less sick, but it didn't. He still hacked up blood and winced with pain. It was a Sunday and the rain knocked hard against the picture windows.

"Will you look at that?" My mom opened the shutters. "A double rainbow. My word, I've never seen such a thing. Jon, get George!"

I carried George over to the hospital bed by the window.

"Well, I never," he said.

The storm divided the sky in two: powder blue and black. On the light patch, two prisms arched parallel with each other while the black sparked with lightning and stirred with thunder. We all watched the weather show until the rainbows dissolved into sunlight. When I tried to move George back into his La-Z-Boy, he held out his hand and said, "I think I'm gonna stay here." I lifted his legs and helped him roll onto his back.

That night my mom had to work and I knew Maria wasn't coming over anytime soon, so I pulled the La-Z-Boy over to the hospital bed. George's head rested on two pillows, his eyes were closed, and his breath was shallow. Knowing the end was near, I allowed myself to drink in his presence and I heard myself slur.

"George, you're a good man."

His eyes remained closed, but I believed he heard me.

"You're like a monument. You came in and gave us consistency. I appreciate that. There were times when I feared you. But it wasn't like the fear I had when it was just my mom and me. It was respect. You took us in and taught me manners."

I snuck a sip and then I stopped myself. I could feel a tremble in the back of my legs and a twitch in my right eye.

"You never know who will take care of you," he replied. Then his body heaved and I handed him the bucket.

I passed out in the La-Z-Boy. The pain in my head trumped the stiffness in my back and neck from sleeping upright. I opened my eyes and noticed the sun from the shutters sprayed directly on George's face. His eyes were closed, but his flesh had collapsed like the outside of a rotting pumpkin. His head was thrown back and his lower jaw dropped. His mouth was wide open. I walked over and cupped one hand under his chin and the other on his forehead and closed his mouth.

Seeing George empty like that scared me. It made me think that we just go dark. I pulled the sheet over his head and angled the shutters so the perfect amount of light shined on his body. The pattern looked like piano keys. I stayed there until the rays of light moved from his body onto my face. I thought about the picture I saw in the *Dallas Times* of Scarlett and her new husband, Zack and his studio in LA, about the phone calls that I would have to make to my mother and Betty and Bill. I thought about how I didn't think about Maria. I sat there breathing it all in, until the sun warmed my face. I don't know how long I sat there. Could've been minutes or hours, but I didn't move away from it and get a drink.

TEMPORARY THING

They met Henry at the Sundance Film Festival. Mae and Carter were the only non-industry people at a wine bar on Main Street. Bored, they overpaid for some pills. The ecstasy hit Mae as Henry entered the room. Every cell of her body lined up as if she felt herself expecting him.

"You hated it," she said over the loud music.

"Excuse me?" Henry looked confused.

"Don't mind her," Carter said. "She's an only child. She can be very direct."

"Admit it. You hated what they did with your script. I could tell by your body language on stage. You didn't even want to be up there."

A disdainful look spread across Henry's face. He wondered if everyone in the audience had seen his contempt. Before he could respond, Monica, a producer with dreadlocks, grabbed his arm. "Let's get out of here," she said. "The cast-only party is at Mika's house. If we don't leave now, the car might not make it with all the snow."

Henry looked dubiously at Mae, a tall and slender brunette. She sat with perfect posture: no elbows on the table, her hands resting on her lap, her legs crossed at the ankle. Yet she tapped her right foot feverishly as if she was waiting for something. Henry held Mae's gaze as the wait staff moved around them, passing appetizers and holding trays of wine.

Carter watched the two of them looking at each other and held his breath. He felt for Henry. He'd listened to him explain, on stage, that he'd worked on this movie for over four years. Not only had he written the script but it was based on his novel, a novel that had taken him over a decade to finish.

"Are you coming?" Monica tugged on Henry's sleeve.

"I'll catch up with you later," Henry said. "I've just met some old friends."

Henry's manners and slow drawl disarmed Carter, and he momentarily stopped thinking of him as a threat. The way that he handled himself earned him an introduction to Mae Ryder.

"Take a seat," Carter said, as he pulled out a chair. "You are our first guest."

"On what?" Henry sat down.

"Why, *The Mae and Carter Show*," Mae laughed, feeling satisfied.

"Is this some kind of blog?" Henry scowled, fearing he'd made a dreadful mistake.

"No, we loathe blogs," Mae said. "They cheapen every interaction. Dilute the English language. It's journal writing made public without care or revision."

"So, you're an editor," Henry spoke to Mae.

"God no," she said. "I'm just an observer."

"Don't believe a word she tells you," Carter replied. "She's in sales. Paid her way through college selling books."

"Is that true?" Henry perked up.

"Number one in my region," Mae replied.

"Let me guess? Somewhere outside LA?"

"Not even close," said Mae. "Chesterfield, South Carolina."

"I know exactly where it is. I'm from Savannah," Henry spoke with a new depth in his voice.

Henry fell into their banter as if he'd written their play and they were rehearsing his lines. He could not tell if Mae and Carter had slept together, were sleeping together, or had never slept together at all.

That intrigued him. He missed real people, people who talked to have conversation, not to get a movie deal out of him.

Mae placed a turquoise pill in his hand. It had been 20-something years since he'd taken a pill this color; but when the girl—and yes, he thought, she was still a girl—squeezed it into his hand, he took it without hesitation.

"Has anyone ever told you that you look like an actress?" Henry flagged for a waitress.

"Have they..." Carter said under his breath.

"You're too young to actually be her. But she was in a couple of films in the '80s. One of them I quite ..."

The waitress interrupted and Henry ordered a Jack and Coke. "Less than Zero. That's the movie. What was her name?"

"Jamie Gertz," Carter said, blankly. "She looks like a young Jamie Gertz."

"Thank you." Henry spoke to both Carter and the waitress, who'd brought him his drink. He took out his reading glasses and looked at the red leather menu.

"You won't be hungry by the time the food arrives." Mae's pupils were almost as big as her irises. She lifted her arms and twisted her hair into a bun. Carter observed the beauty and the horror of her hair: she had a lot of it, layers and layers of thick brown curls. Corkscrews littered her neck and shoulders. He wanted to pluck them off one by one, and he would have, if he didn't already know that she would've slapped his wrist.

"Would you sign my book?" Mae took her copy out of her purse and sarcastically said, "They're giving them away at the door. Is that a bad sign?"

"That they're souvenirs?" Henry took out his pen. "Books are now just promotions for the movie. A relic. People take them home as door stoppers. Never to be opened again."

"We promise to read it." Mae looked at Carter to chime in. She glared at him, but he'd missed his cue.

Carter gulped down his glass of water and, with a shaky hand, he poured himself another. The first wave of the drug hit his delicate stomach—hard. He told himself that this too would pass. Mae shot him a "keep your cool" glance that only made things more terrible. He knew how awful she would be if he messed this up for her. He took long deep breaths out of his nose and a small sigh crept from his mouth.

"Excuse me," he said to a waitress. "Could we get some more water? No bubbles, please." Carter steadied his eyes on Mae's Egyptian blue dress. Its silk wrapped around her torso and draped down her legs.

"After you sold the script," Mae said, "did they allow you on set, or is it like giving your child away for adoption—you never see them again?"

"Oh, you get visitation privileges," Henry paused. "But it's no longer yours. You just birth it. Then it has a life of its own. A cast and crew who influence it. A director, who thinks she knows how to raise it better than you. A cinematographer, who has his own ideas. And you, the creator, are basically forgotten and asked around once or twice out of charity."

"I guess it's all part of the process," Mae said.

"It is," Henry said, "but not one without regrets."

When the waitress returned, Carter regained his composure, and the conversation turned to literature. As the guys discussed Turgenev, Mae sat quietly, enjoying her high, listening to the sound her tights made as she crossed and uncrossed her legs. And just when Henry thought she was an accessory, she would say something about each book. "I've always thought Bazarov was onto something with his nihilism. Social order and traditional values are strange, passed down beliefs. Perhaps only art has meaning. Yet, when I saw you on stage I wondered if even art is an illusion. To keep us going, you know. To believe that *something* we do is important.

"I think Bazarov was more of a nihilist in the sense of revolutionary reform," Carter jumped in, fearing Mae had offended Henry. She often acted too intimate with people before she knew them well enough.

"More people know about Defoe than Turgenev," Henry replied, yet it was clear that he was still thinking about what Mae had said.

"Moll Flanders," Mae laughed. "What a whore! Yet still a hero? The most unhappy of all women. I'd rather die young and be poisoned like Bazarov than have a lifetime like that."

"Bazarov was not poisoned," Henry said. "He died of the plague."

"It was typhus," Carter corrected him. "He got it from a peasant."

"Same thing," Mae said. "Cigarettes! That's what we need—cigarettes."

Henry's body started to tingle—the rush—this was his favorite part. His problems drained down his legs and he checked to see if there was a large puddle under his chair. He laughed at the dry checkered floor. He found himself thinking, and then saying out loud, one of Blake's poems, " Cruelty has a human heart, and jealousy a human face; terror the human form divine, and Secrecy the human dress."

"The drugs must be kicking in," Mae grinned.

"She always dismisses poetry," Carter spoke to Henry. "There was a time when poetry moved a few softer hearts." Carter frowned, sourly. He liked Blake's poem. He knew it well. What he didn't like was that Henry was the one reciting it to her. Mae laughed again at something

Henry had said. Carter would patent her laughter if he could.

When Mae finally smoked a cigarette outside, Henry suggested that they all go to the after-party. Mae sat in between Carter and Henry in the cab, running her hands along her tights while Carter bit at his lips. The driver kept glancing at them in the rearview mirror. They had to be someone. The driver could just tell. The older man's brown hair was styled, messy. He had that well-preserved look that only Hollywood could buy. His velvet blazer, purple shirt, and gray cashmere scarf screamed self-importance. The girl's curly brown hair fell past her shoulders. She had glowing ivory skin and unnaturally white teeth. One of those wider jaws with a pointy chin and a long distinguished nose. She listened to the older man, probably a movie director of some sort, but kept looking at herself in the mirror. The cab driver couldn't tell if her cheekbones were actually that high or if she was sucking the inside of her mouth in to make it appear that way.

Suddenly, the girl screamed and pointed to the brightest star in the sky. They all looked out the window and the younger guy, the one who looked the least enthused, said flatly, "That's Venus."

"Named after the Roman goddess of love and beauty," the cab driver chimed in, but they only smiled. Now that he looked closer, they seemed slightly off, like they were on something.

This was the driver's 15th film festival and he began to notice these sorts of things. He never watched the movies. Didn't care. But he did like to impress his wife, who, after the festival was over, showed him pictures in the grocery store magazines of all the famous people who invaded Main Street for one week once a year. He would point to this one and that one and say, "Yeah, those two were in my cab." "No way!" she'd howl. "How did they look? What were they wearing? Were they nice? How much did they tip?"

Thinking of his wife, the driver adjusted the rearview mirror. Still, nothing. But there was something about the older man's voice that haunted him. It was shaky and low with the cadence of a poet telling a ghost story. He knew he'd heard it before, yet he couldn't place it. He turned down the talk radio.

"In Savannah," Henry said, "neighbors would gather around the front porch and tell stories. When I moved to Manhattan, I missed those warm sultry nights filled with fireflies and laughter. I missed it so much that I recreated it in my living room. Turns out, I wasn't the only one who missed it. Soon we outgrew my small apartment and moved into bars, then theaters, and just by word of mouth every show started selling out. You must come to New York for one of our shows."

"We should. Shouldn't we, Carter?"

"You're on NPR," Carter said. "I've heard one of your podcasts."

"Yes, we've gotten quite big."

"I knew it!" the cab driver said. "I've heard you on the radio."

Henry listened to the driver as he told them about growing up in Utah, selling his ski business, and the depression that followed after he'd stayed home. The driver enjoyed driving a cab, mostly because he never knew where he'd end up. You start your night in one place and end up in another. It's completely out of your control. You surrender to the night. It was the first time he'd ever been able to do that.

"Have you ever thought about telling your story in public?" Henry leaned forward.

"Me?" the cab driver replied. "Never dreamt of it."

"You should consider it." Henry took out his card. "Email me if you're ever in New York."

As the cab stopped, Henry thanked the driver, gave him a generous tip, and stepped out. To help Mae over the ice, he held her hand and she did not let go as they walked up the long salted driveway.

Carter followed, droopy-eyed, kicking clumps of snow. It was cold enough to see their breath. Cold enough to pack a perfect snowball and hit Henry in the head. He put his hands in his pockets and walked into the line of entitled filmmakers, publicists, and agents waiting to get into the party.

As they walked past the crowd into a grove of Aspen trees, Mae looked up and marveled at the perfect white triangles on top of the Wasatch Mountains. She couldn't see where they were going. It looked like people were standing in a line to get into a forest. Just then, two Hollywood searchlights crisscrossed and illuminated the outline of a house hidden by the narrow trees. Mae stopped in the snow, squinting to see through the branches. She saw a low, extended building with wide overhanging eaves and wood bands. She guessed the house was built during the late 20s to early 30s, and she grabbed her phone to check. No. She stopped herself. Avoid the light-up screen. Trust your intuition. The house was carved into nature. It had to be his. Her heart raced with recognition when she identified the prairie school home.

"Do you know what we're walking into?" she asked, dropping Henry's hand and running back to Carter.

"Can someone tell me what's happening?" Henry asked.

"It is," she said. "It really is. I can't fucking believe it."

She danced around Carter, her elbows pointing to the sky, her long neck pecking. She looked like an off-beat chicken. When Carter understood, he celebrated by stamping out an imaginary cigarette and let the twist travel up his leg and into his hips.

"Can someone please tell me what is going on?" Henry repeated, as angry as one can be on ecstasy.

"It appears that we're walking into a Frank Lloyd Wright house," Carter said. "He's her favorite."

"It's so incredible," Mae said. "I can't believe we get to go inside."

Henry felt confused and left out. He missed the warmth of Mae's hand.

"She was an architectural history major," Carter explained. "This is her thing."

"Carter," Mae stopped herself. She didn't have to say anything else. He knew how much this meant to her. How much she idolized the architect. How this had to be a sign. She'd read everything about him, had his sketches on postcards in her room, and she'd even visited Oak Park in Illinois to see his home and studio.

"This is wild," she said. "What are the chances?"

Mae linked arms with Carter and Henry and the three of them skipped past the disgruntled people on their phones and headed to the front of the line. Both men were happy—they held Mae's arms and through osmosis they experienced her optimism. They charged at the bouncer in the puffy Sundance Film Festival jacket and right before Henry opened his mouth he said, "I don't care who you are. Everyone in this line is on the list. We're at capacity. You'll have to go to the back."

Mae looked at Carter. Now what? Her eyes shook. The line was too long. They would never get in even if they waited all night. Carter put his arm around Mae and she placed her head on his shoulder.

"At least we got to see it," he whispered, "it's freezing. Let's just go back to the hotel."

Henry pulled an invitation out of his back pocket and handed it to the bouncer. "I am Henry Warren Scott and this is my film." He pointed to his name. The bouncer called someone on his walkie-talkie and said, "Just two of you." Henry grabbed for Mae's hand and she paused in front of the giant Hollywood machine that hummed and sprayed light into the trees. Carter jammed his hands in his pockets. He would walk away. Take a cab back to their shared hotel room with double beds that he'd paid for, pack his bags, and get on the first flight in the morning. This time he'd keep his word. He'd never talk to her again. Block her number. Ignore her charm. But just before he stormed away, he heard her say to the bouncer, "Come on. We're all together."

Mae gave the bouncer her most inviting smile. She projected all her attention onto him. Two caramel beams assuring springtime in the dead of winter. The bouncer looked straight ahead, unaffected, and she nervously played with her hair. Then, as if he'd heard her small town heart pleading, he melted and said, "Alright, go in."

The bouncer lifted the velvet rope and Henry, Mae, and Carter strolled into the warm room filled with celebrities wearing humble artist masks. Mae glided through the house, her fingertips tracing the textured moldings. She counted the clerestory windows. Noted the horizontal lines and open space. "Coming into this house would be something like putting on your hat and going outdoors." Yes, she thought. It feels exactly like that. She looked up at the low-pitch roof—"Hello," she whispered, high as a kite. She knew that she'd get here eventually. Experience things that she'd read about in books. But why did she have so much anxiety when she was so close to the things she wanted?

"I love your work," a man's voice startled her. She thought he had mistaken her for an actress until she turned around and realized that he was speaking to another gentleman.

"No, I love your work!" the man with tortoiseshell glasses replied. "You are brilliant."

"No, you're brilliant! You look amazing. Tell me, are you Gluten-free?"

"How'd you know?"

"You just have that glow about you."

"Bet you win the Grand Jury Prize."

"Whatever you do," the man with the tortoiseshell glasses said, "you have to be your own boss. You must have all creative control. Everyone in that Godforsaken town is influenced by the imitations. No one knows the originals, you know?"

Mae wanted to jump in, say something about Turgenev and Wright, but she was a nobody. She smiled as she walked past them, her hand touching the wall. She had to sit down. She pulled Carter over to the timber and stone fireplace and took off her shoes.

"I wouldn't have gone in without you," she said in her sweetest voice, but neither of them believed it.

"You look scared," he replied.

"I am. I'm afraid they're going to sniff me out. Like at any moment, someone is going to tap me on my shoulder and ask me to leave."

"Well, you look the part."

"Yeah, but I'm a phony. I've created nothing of value."

"You just got into graduate school. That's something."

"That doesn't count. It's just an insecure pursuit for validation." Mae looked into the fireplace that Frank Lloyd Wright had built and said, "I know you're older than me, but you're too comfortable." She paused. "You're doing too well. They keep promoting you, giving you more money. I'm not telling you to give it up, I'm just saying write something on the side."

"I get to travel," Carter said with contempt. "I get to see things. Last month I was in Pakistan. Plus, I don't want to add to the drivel. Everyone's a writer now. If I wrote anything serious, I'd want to write a masterpiece."

"You sound like Flaubert," Mae rolled her eyes. "You've already rewritten Death Room II, you might as well retire."

Carter laughed and leaned into Mae; regardless how self-serving she could be, there was still no one he'd rather be with. The two sat huddled together like lovers (or was it only good friends?) when Henry found them with two glasses of champagne.

"We were just talking about Carter's successful career as a script doctor before journalism," Mae put her hand on Carter's leg.

"You're a writer as well." Henry handed the glass of champagne to Mae. "I knew you were a man of words."

"I'm mostly a publisher now."

"He writes a column once a month and has, like, a million followers," Mae interjected.

"And what about you, Mae Ryder, what do you do?"

"I already told you. I'm in sales."

"Or better yet, what do you want to do?"

"Let's see," she put her finger to her lips. "Direct a movie. Act. Something in fashion. So I'm going back to school."

"I never went to college," Henry replied.

"Not just any school," Carter pressed, "Parsons School of Design, majoring in...what is it again?"

"Decorative arts," Mae said.

"You want to be an interior designer?" Henry sounded disappointed. "You just said that you wanted to direct films, act, be in fashion."

"Interiors don't scare me."

"Huh," Henry said, still looking let down.

"Let's not talk about the future," she felt another wave of the drug hitting her. "Let's just sit here, enjoying each other. Henry, tell us more about your life. Who was the first girl that you ever kissed?"

Mae stretched out her arms and listened to Henry's story about kissing Gretchen Gilmore in the parking lot of the Piggly Wiggly. She loved a good story, and Henry had created an entire business around storytelling. Carter traveled the world writing down other people's stories, and Mae sat around high, listening to them. It was no big surprise that they all found each other. It was also the reason why the trio would remain friends many years after. That, and both men were curious how Mae's life would play out. They wondered if she would do something herself or if she was a genuine muse.

Mae started to sit up straight when she felt someone new noticing her. He was scrawny with alabaster skin. His whole demeanor exuded superiority. His black and white striped shirt clung to his skin, exposing his pale hips sliding into leather pants. She slowly put on her heels and excused herself to the bathroom, walking right past him, without so much as a glance. Henry's expression shifted from amusing to suspicious.

"That was abrupt," Henry said.

"Maybe she's feeling ill," Carter covered for Mae.

As conciliation, Carter told Henry about his trip to Islamabad, the architecture of the Saudi-Pak Tower, the view from the Sharkarparian hills, and the diversity of Pakistani culture and religions. Henry slowly returned to his animated self. His eyes moved up and down as if he were reading notes across a scale, giving Carter the impression that he felt every word. Carter had never been in the presence of someone so attentive, except for maybe in his early 20s when he was in therapy. Maybe his life had meaning. Maybe it wasn't *all* pointless.

The two men were so engrossed with each other that they almost forgot about Mae Ryder. The musicians played their guitars and sang campfire songs in a circle. Henry loathed their whiny music and headed outside for some air, but Carter found their harmonies angelic. The two boys, the skinny one whom Mae pretended to ignore, and the kid next to him with the soft curly hair, had to be brothers to blend their voices like that. Other people joined the circle, young starlets and cultish celebrities, who looked anything but ordinary in real life. Mae sat amongst them. She sang quietly so no one could hear her voice and luckily, no one clapped to make her off cue. Carter watched her play coy by twirling her finger in her thick hair.

When Carter joined the circle he did not sit next to Mae. He sat across from her and released his falsetto from his days with the boys' choir at boarding school. The voice registered so high that the two rockstar cousins lifted their limp heads to smirk at each other. *Was this guy kidding?* He was so committed that they almost lost it, and if Mae weren't on the Jesus-drug she would've laughed with them, but because the ecstasy still pulsed in her blood she smiled at Carter without exposing any intimacy between them. She turned it on and off at her disposal. There were so many sides of her in one body. She managed to entertain all of her suitors without ever giving herself away.

Mae channeled all her energy to the lead singer. Carter walked over to where Henry sat with two very young blonde girls, who giggled and snuggled into each other, actresses wanting to star in Henry's next thriller. Carter suddenly longed to clean his teeth, put on his pajama bottoms, and finish re-reading Nabokov's *Glory*. "Meet my friend Carter," Henry said to the girls, waving him over. "He's a writer as well."

"Is he?" one of them asked, fixing her blouse.

He held up his hand to acknowledge the invitation, but politely declined. The ecstasy sank him into the couch and poured lead into his boots. His eyes darted between Mae and the musician and Henry and the girls. His thought was so loud that he wondered if he said it out loud. "Power corrupts," he thought, "even sexual power." Yet young women have so few other powers in our society. He looked at Mae compassionately, then contemptuously. If you have control of this temporary thing, you'd be an idiot not to use it. Everyone in this room was wrestling for it, in some way or another. What pretty young human wouldn't use it under the circumstances? You'd have to be a saint. And who ever loved a saint?

Henry slid between the two girls and the musician sang only for Mae. In between songs, Mae laughed at something the musician said. The familiar weight of jealousy pressed on Carter's abdomen as he watched her do her thing, this time, with the musician. He picked up his heavy shoe and crossed his leg. He decided he would ask his girlfriend back home to marry him. Mae got up and walked to the bathroom. The singer put down his guitar and followed her. This time, she looked over her shoulder at him and smiled, gloriously. The boy with the soft curls didn't even lift his head. His fingers pressed lightly on the strings as Carter sang in his falsetto, alone.

AMME

On the first day of yoga teacher training, we sat in a circle reciting our names, our favorite yoga pose, and an explanation of what had brought us there. Amme stood out immediately because she was the tannest white person in the room, which wasn't saying much for San Francisco. Still, Amme looked as if she spent hours a day devoted to the sun in a city that hardly broke 65 degrees.

I couldn't guess her age. It could've been anywhere between 25 and 35. The silver glitter smeared across her eyelids made me think she was under 30. Or perhaps she used the glitter to conceal her age? I found her strangely beautiful and a touch masculine: her arms were muscular, her pecs flat, and her legs defined.

"And why are *you* here?" the teacher asked Amme just as a wiry young man skulked through the double doors carrying a piece of wood.

"Excuse me." The teacher waved him over. "This is Ryan. He's already been through our program. He's refinishing the loft upstairs so we will have a meditation room. He may be practicing with us throughout our training. Everyone say hello to Ryan."

"Hello Ryan," the group chanted back.

"I'm sorry. Where were we? Oh yes, Amme...why are you here?"

"To deepen my practice," Amme said, looking seductively at Ryan. "My favorite posture is Pincha Mayurasana."

"Does anyone know what Pincha Mayurasana is?" the teacher over-enunciated the Sanskrit only Amme used.

"It's an elbow stand, right?" I asked, even though I already knew it was correct.

"Yes." The teacher looked pleased. "And what's your name?"

"Me?" She'd jumped across the circle. I hadn't thought of my answers yet. There were still 12 people ahead of me. "Oh, I'm...I'm... Emma. My favorite pose is, well, I guess I never thought about it."

I could not think of another pose. Couldn't remember what any of them were called. I wanted to say the same one as Amme, because it was my favorite pose, but I didn't want to look like I was copying her.

"Tree pose?" I said finally. A safe and boring balance posture.

"Vrksasana," the teacher said. "And what brings you here?"

I didn't really know why I was there. So many things had changed in a short amount of time: I'd gotten married, changed my name, my address, and a few months later I lost my job. I'd lost my identity and now I found myself in a cross-legged position, repeating Sanskrit. I looked up and counted the number of skylights in the large warehouse that I'd been going to a couple times a week for the last year. Seven. There were seven.

"To learn more about yoga?" I said.

"Okay." She pointed to the woman beside me.

After class, I told Amme that I liked Pincha Mayurasana, too, but that I could only do it against the wall. At first, she seemed unenthused, but then later she invited me over to her house for a party.

"Call me," she said, running out to a guy I assumed must be her husband waiting in a two-seater Porsche convertible.

"But I don't know your number!"

"It's 786-AMME."

"Really?" I asked, but she was already gone.

Amme lived on the third floor of an old Victorian, one block west of the Haight-Ashbury intersection. A narrow hallway led me up flight after flight of stairs until I walked into a crowded living room buzzing with people. Amme, dressed in white—from boa, to mini-skirt, to fishnet stockings, to her go-go boots—greeted me immediately. She introduced me to her husband Tony, who had wrinkles around his eyes, and his face made about six different smiles upon meeting me.

"You see, Tony, not all people who do yoga are a bunch of freaks," Amme said. "Emma, let me get you a drink." She walked to the bar, swaying her hips.

Tony started to quiz me on the yoga program. I told him there were 23 women and two men who were a couple. This fact seemed to please him. He seemed to be concerned by how much time Amme had been spending at the studio. He asked what I planned to do after the program ended. I explained that I was only taking this training as a gift to myself before I started looking for another job. "To be honest," I said. "I don't really know what I'm doing. For the first time in my life I feel a little lost." He nodded to himself and said he hoped Amme would return to practicing law.

Amme was a lawyer? I hadn't imagined that.

"I'm a journalist," I said, "At least until my magazine shut down and the bad people came in and confiscated our computers."

Tony's mouth twitched.

"I wish I could practice in India," I said. "But now that I'm married, I can't just pack up and travel by myself anymore. You know?"

The smiling stopped. I could tell by the look on Tony's face he didn't know what I was talking about. He'd married at 40. He'd probably traveled the world by himself. Slept with a good number of people. Had made his own money. I supposed he wanted to coast into codependency and do everything with Amme now.

"And where is your husband tonight?" Tony asked.

"He's at the Giant's game tonight."

"Well, bring him over next time."

"I will," I lied. "Next time."

Amme handed me a glass of champagne. She put her arm around my waist and introduced me to her clan: Dr. Schwartz, an amateur filmmaker and physician, who ran a private practice for "people who don't want to deal with insurance;" Laurent and Colette, a bohemian French couple who now traveled around the U.S. in a mobile home while selling their oil paintings; and Xavier, a local jazz performer who often played impromptu sets at the Boom Boom Room on Fillmore.

"Get your coat," Amme squealed over the music, "I'm going to the bathroom. I'll meet you at the back door." I found my black wool coat and patiently waited as Amme instructed. When she returned, she wore a perm-a-grin smile and her eyes were large and white like golf balls. She wrapped herself in her white rabbit fur and said, "Follow me. Watch your step."

The roof deck contained one rusty lawn chair and a horde of dehydrated plants, but the view of Ashbury Heights made it enchanting. I turned over a plastic pail and sat down. Amme lit my American Spirit.

"Your name," she said, "is my name spelled backwards. My horoscope told me I would meet someone. Do you want me to read your palm?"

"Sure." She grabbed my long fingers.

"It's too dark up here. I'll read it later."

"I like your coat," I said.

"It was Mama's. She wore it on the day she met my Daddy, who was 27 years older. Mama always says I have his nose and each year for my birthday, she offers to pay to get my nose and boobs done. You see, Mama got both her nose and boobs done after she divorced Daddy and moved to Marin, where she finally got what she always wanted—a billionaire. It only took her three marriages. I stayed in Mobile until Daddy died in my arms at 80. After that, I lost a lover to suicide. I had nowhere else to go except to Marin with Mama. That's when I met Tony and moved in here. He and his friends sort of adopted me."

Amme told me her entire life story in one sweeping breath from Mobile to San Francisco to marrying Tony in a bathroom on acid, then later, having a ceremony at City Hall and a party at her Mama's house in Marin. Looking childlike buried in fur, she christened me her new best friend then said, "Shit! I forgot about the brownies in the oven." She flicked her cigarette on the deck. Our time was over. We climbed down the stairs, clutching the splintered rail.

I could hardly wait the two days until I saw Amme at the yoga studio. I wanted to ask her if Laurent and Colette painted the abstract at the bottom of the stairs. Did Dr. Schwartz treat one of the band members of R.E.M. for that rumored overdose? But Amme did not sit next to me in the circle. At the break, there were no private jokes shared or affection of any kind. She seemed like a different person. Her face appeared less vibrant, as if her skin was pale underneath a tanned mask and her eyes looked puffy and dark.

I ran up to Amme after practice. "What time did everyone leave on Saturday?"

"They didn't," she mumbled.

"Like, everyone slept over? How fun."

"More like, we didn't sleep."

Ryan walked down the stairs. Amme's eyes followed him.

"I have to go," she said.

"Where are you going?"

"I just have to go ...but we'll have another party on Friday."

"I'll be there," I said, a little too loudly.

At the party, Amme greeted me with an exaggerated warmth, "Hello! Everyone," she announced, "this is Emma. The only cool girl in my yoga program." She twirled me around. "Damn, your ass looks good in those pants." Then she was off, getting something for someone: a drink, warm socks, a Band-Aid. Later, I'd overhear her telling a new person about her dead ex-boyfriend and how she'd finished her law degree and passed two state bars on speed. She told the same stories, over and over again, to new listeners, as if she hoped someone would understand her, but they never did. No one did. But everyone enjoyed being around her.

I soon learned that Amme loved strangers, liked acquaintances, and didn't have any friends. She replaced friends with audiences, people who listened to her monologues on various topics ranging from her passion for tomatoes to the one book she read on Japanese Shogun. I found myself waiting to have my time with her. Why this was important to me, I did not know.

On Monday, Amme ate lunch on the lawn of the Yerba Buena Garden and invited me to join her. I walked under the cascading Martin Luther King Jr. Waterfall and read his reassuring words etched in the glass wall: "The ultimate measure of a man is not where he stands in moments of comfort and convenience, but where he stands at times of challenge and controversy." It was a beautiful place to be quiet and reflect. As soon as I walked out, I heard Amme's loud voice. "I've lost my credit card," she yelled across the lawn, then to the agent. "Martha Mills. Martha Ammons Mills. Martha A-M-M-O-N-S Mills."

As soon as she got off the phone I said, "Your name is Martha Mills?"

"Huh?"

"It's like finding out Bob Dylan is really Robert Zimmerman or that Carmen Electra is really Tara Gross. It's disorienting."

"What's your maiden name?"

"Cavanaugh," I said slowly. "I should have kept it. Have you always gone by Amme?"

"No," she said, pulling a pencil and a Granny Smith apple out of her bag. "In Mobile, I went by Martha but when I moved out here, it just hit me—I Am Me." She spat the apple stem on the grass. "Is Carmen Electra really Tara Gross?"

"No, but it's Tara something."

Behind my sunglasses, I watched Amme use the pencil like a scalpel. She carved a tunnel through the apple's core. Then she stabbed the apple and twisted the pencil until the second incision diagonally met the first. She stuffed reddish herb into the core, pressed her mouth to the second hole, lit the top, and let out a cloud of smoke. A sweet aroma filled the air. A pink kiss was planted on the green apple.

I'd never seen anyone turn an apple into a pipe, nor did I know it was possible. I acted as if it was as ordinary as opening a can of soda. She hit the apple again and the ebb and flow of her thoughts seemed to flatline. I watched as she absorbed everything around her: the flowering trees, the evergreen shrubs, the Wisteria covered loggia. She mentioned something about receiving wisdom from the trees. That they were alive. Then she picked up a rock. "Look at this," she said. "To us, it's just a rock but at a subatomic level, it is moving, dancing, changing." Then she passed me the apple and I politely declined.

"Don't touch the stuff," I smiled. "It makes me paranoid."

Amme shrugged her shoulders and took another hit.

Pot shut me down. I hated losing track of words, being openly lost. It was very important to me to at least appear as if I had things together. But a contact high with Amme gave me the expansiveness of the drug—without the paranoia. I listened to her talk more about the trees, how she liked meditating in nature, and how she received energy from the earth. At the time, I'd not heard of such things. The March sun warmed my forehead. I took off my jacket and Amme and I reclined on the grass.

At the third or fourth party (they all seemed to blend into one long night), I wandered into Tony's office and found a small group gathering around in what Amme called the Zen Lounge. The room was painted a vermillion red and all the furniture sat low to the floor.

"Come in," Amme said. "Shut the door behind you."

I thought they must be playing a board game until I saw beyond the purple spray orchid. They flocked like gray pigeons: Tony, Dr. Schwartz, Xavier, Laurent, and Colette. One lengthy snort after another. Then they wiped their noses and headed down the hallway. It appeared devilishly glamorous in the candlelit room, ambient music playing, surrounded by attractive and healthy faces. The yoga program preached about "accepting what the universe brings you." I doubted the universe was referring to this.

"Want some?" Tony offered.

"Why not?" I said.

"Don't worry, sweetie-baby," Amme said. "You can stay here as long as you like."

"I need to be home at midnight."

Amme took the ponytail holder off her wrist and tied my hair back, then she handed me a purple straw. The lambskin rug felt soft on my knees as I hunched over the coffee table.

Somebody turned up the music. "I like this song," I said, walking down the hall. I felt the urge to dance. A few girls were in the center of the room. Before I thought they were strange but now I was brave enough to join them. It felt nice to move. The room warmed up and I threw my sweater on the couch.

Yoga changed my body completely. I stood taller, no longer embarrassed about having a chest, my limbs leaner. I lifted my arms and felt my tank top rise, exposing my hip bones and belly. The music picked up. More bodies filled the floor. I closed my eyes. My ponytail brushed my back like a pendulum. What time was it?

"Do you want a cigarette?" Amme yelled across the room as she pointed to the stairs.

More than anything, I thought.

"Didn't you say you had to be home?"

"Nah, I'll go home later."

By 9:00 am on Monday, we'd sweated all the toxins out. We were learning the Primary Series, the first 72 postures in the Ashtanga yoga sequence, which took about two hours if you included all five backbends and the finishing head and shoulder stands. It was like pressing the restart button. My mind felt clear and uncomplicated. I don't remember when Ryan started practicing with us. Maybe he was always there? But I noticed him when Amme and I moved to the back corner. Some days she would place her purple mat across from him. Other days they'd practice side by side. Then one day, I heard them breathe, in unison, the entire 72 postures.

Savasana, corpse pose, ended the practice. The teacher left us in the steamy room, flat on our backs with our palms up, floating. Unable to be still, Amme would pop up and give me an adjustment, then Ryan. She stood over me and put her hands under my shoulder blades and pulled them down my back. Then she sat on the floor and pressed her feet into my shoulders, cradled my head, and lengthened my neck until the last bit of tension released, making me feel shapeless. She'd work quickly on me, and lingered over Ryan.

After practice, Amme would go upstairs to help Ryan with the meditation room. She claimed to have an interest in interiors. They'd smoke a joint and she would help him hang curtains, snap chalk lines, and even install the bathroom sink. When I'd walk up the spiral staircase, they'd always be slightly touching.

This time it was shoulder to shoulder. Amme held a piece of wood while Ryan cut a two-by-four. Ryan, in his blue jeans and old T-shirt, turned off the electric saw and removed his glasses.

"Hello, beautiful," he said. "Do you want to smoke a fatty?"

"Not today," I blushed.

"Come on," Ryan leaned toward me.

"No," Amme insisted. "Pot is not good for her. She gets paranoid."

"Are you packed?" Ryan exhaled, while Amme started to giggle.

"Are we going somewhere?" I tried to play along.

"We're going to Utah," Ryan said.

"Why Utah?"

"Polygamy is legal in Utah." Ryan laughed with Amme.

"I don't get it."

"Amme was telling me you were having some problems with your husband."

"She was, was she?"

I looked at Amme with both understanding and confusion. I never told her I was having problems with my husband. But she must have known I was avoiding him, like someone who avoids the dentist, but knows that they will eventually have to lay in the chair, open their mouth, and place the rubbery mask over their nose and inhale the laughing gas.

"I thought Uncle Ryan could help you both out."

I shook my head at them. "Let's go," I teased. "Let's go to Utah."

On the days Amme wasn't with Ryan, we sat on the grass and listened to the Martin Luther King, Jr. Waterfall. European tourists, the homeless, and businessmen and women shared the landscaped lawn. I used to be one of those people in a blue suit, only allowed sunshine for 20 minutes before I had to return to my cubicle. But now I was barefoot, my toenails painted a sparkly silver, my chest flushed and freckled from too much sun, leisurely enjoying my lunch. I wondered if I would ever go back.

Like kids, Amme and I did handstands and backbends in the grass. Amme could do drop-backs by herself. She started standing in Tadasana, her feet hips-distance apart, her hands in prayer at her chest.

She pressed her hips forward and arched her back until it looked like she would come crashing down on the top of her head. Then, gracefully, she extended her arms and her hands touched the ground only for a moment or two before her thighs pulled her back up to standing.

Backbending was an endorphin rush. We'd learned that it increased energy and decreased depression, and we experienced it firsthand. Even though the body was stagnant, the heart raced as if it had just run a 100-yard dash. Some days, we'd do ten of them in a row just to feel good. I couldn't do drop-backs by myself. Amme spotted me. She put her leg between my legs and held my hips while I reached for the ground. Once my hands hit the earth, she pulled me upright.

One weekend a year, the cops barricade off six blocks for the Haight Street Fair. I remember Amme wore blue, glittery, star-shaped sunglasses and I tucked my blonde hair into a short pink wig. She thought it would be fun to have a sidewalk sale: old CDs, astrology books, tired boots, a pair of binoculars, and wrinkled clothing littered the Ashbury sidewalk. Tony bought an extra-long speaker cord so we could crank the LCD Soundsystem on the front steps. Dr. Schwartz (whom I now called Andrew) and I welcomed people who stopped over to buy a shirt for a buck or to bum a smoke. I waved a stick with a plastic alligator head on it and collected the money in its mouth. By 3:00 pm, we'd made $11.

With our earnings, we decided to buy bubbly water. Amme, Tony, and I weaved through the crowd that smelled like sweat and hemp to get to the corner store. Amme and Tony held hands while I fell behind, eyeing the grills with rotating corn. That's when I saw Ryan, his long hair, his green-blue eyes, standing in line by himself. In my pink wig and pink shield sunglasses, I was invisible. I watched him watch them. Their hands intertwined, coordinated tans, hips that looked like they matched, and I saw the heartbreak on his face. I felt awful. I wondered what I'd do if I were him. Would I confront them? Would I run? Ryan did not walk any closer. He did not take a second look. He put his money into his pocket and walked uphill with an even pace.

I waited until we closed down the sidewalk sale and Amme and I were alone in her bedroom to tell her about it. Fuck! she said. Then she sat on the bed, tangled her hands in her hair, and pressed her elbows into her stomach.

"I didn't know what to do," I replied. "I felt bad. Like, we betrayed him."

"It's not like he doesn't know that I'm married," she snapped.

"I know. But from what he saw, it looked like you're in love with your husband."

"I love Ryan," she whispered.

"I know."

"I just need some time." She paused. "Some time to say good-bye to Tony."

Just then, the door blew open and Colette and Laurent barged in, double-kissing both our cheeks. Friends of friends from the street fair were drifting into the house and Amme had a whole new audience to entertain. She lectured on astrology, debated theories of reincarnation, and recited the benefits of yoga with an unfamiliar intensity. She also made more trips to the bathroom than usual. I stuck around, waiting for my time with her, wanting to check-in to make sure she was all right. It was after 3:00 am when she finally offered to give me a Tarot reading. Her hands shook as she gave me the cards to shuffle. She looked up the meaning of each card in a miniature book with tiny script and explained how they pertained to my life. When I picked The Pope Upright, she held the book to her chest.

"Emma! The Pope represents anyone who guides us. Like a therapist, a friend, or yoga teacher."

"That's good," I said, hearing what I wanted to hear.

"Don't you see how true the cards are?" She wanted me to believe in Tarot and I was starting to. "The Pope has the ability to listen, not only to the words of others, but to the vibration of all the things that they *don't* say. That's what you do for me. You act as a sounding board. You offer clarity yet you allow me to make up my own mind. You are the only person who doesn't judge me."

I smiled at my friend. Then Amme pressed her face to the tiny book and glanced down. "It says you have a tendency to help others, but..." she paused.

"But what?"

"Oh nothing. The cards aren't always right."

"No. Tell me. Please."

"It says you have the tendency to help others, *but* you often use others to distract you from what's going on inside of you."

My eyes looked away from Amme to Colette's abstract painting on the wall: a gray, silver, and blue confusion. Hopelessness came over me. I wanted to be invisible again. Amme stood up. She said she'd find a Joseph Campbell quote that would further explain my card. She told me to stay there. I waited ten minutes but she never returned. I needed to hear that quote. It felt like my sanity depended on it. I pretended to mingle with the remaining stragglers while looking over their shoulders for Amme. I finally found her in the kitchen.

"What are you doing?" I touched her shoulder.

"Someone spilled juice," she said, placing the pickles, milk, and a carton of eggs on the counter. "I'll be right back."

This time she told the truth. She went to the bathroom and came back with a toothbrush. She ran the raw eggs under cold water, dipped the toothbrush in soap, and scrubbed each one gently so it did not crack. Tony made a comment about how Amme had always been a neat freak and continued his conversation with Xavier.

"Amme, what are you doing?" I panicked. "Are you okay?"

"Why wouldn't I be?" she scowled.

"You're cleaning eggs."

"They're dirty."

"Maybe it's time to go to bed?"

"Maybe it's time you go home to your husband."

The last week of teacher training, I followed Amme into the Yerba Buena Gardens. She sat closer to the waterfall than usual. When I sat down she handed me a brown bag and I broke the avocado sandwich in half while she did her magic on the apple. I picked up the apple and studied it. "Do you mind?"

"Wait," she dug through her duffle bag. "Let me pack it better. You should only smoke the good stuff."

Amme packed the apple with bright red herb from her special bag. Some of the resin landed on my tongue. It tasted spicy yet fruity. I kissed the apple again and instantly the pot enveloped me.

"I want to sit in a hammock on a warm day with someone touching my foot without feeling so awful about it," she said. "I want to stay up all night talking to someone without shoving a bunch of shit up my nose. Does that make me so terrible?"

The pot, which formed an invisible muzzle around my neck and throat, kept me from talking.

"I got caught up in the excitement of getting married," she said, "and I didn't really think it through. Tony doesn't see me. He doesn't know how unhappy I am. How can you be with someone and they can't pick up on your unhappiness? If we were just dating, we would have broken up by now. People break up all the time. Why does it feel like a big fucking failure?"

I leaned forward, my head nodding like a lap dog.

"Ryan broke up with me. Said he didn't want to be responsible for destroying my marriage. Said that we could never have an honest relationship since we met while I was in another relationship." Her eyes started to water and I could feel her heartbreak. Then she spoke with a strange authority, "I'm leaving Tony. I'm moving to New York. I signed up for teacher training there and it starts next week. I've even sublet an apartment."

She poked my wrist, and I found myself watching her poke my wrist. My mouth felt dry.

"You're going?" I asked in disbelief. "Without me?"

"It's like my horoscope said, we will be placeholders for each other," she continued. "We'll always be interconnected. You don't need me. You need to stop being a stranger to yourself."

I frowned. I couldn't believe Amme smoked this shit every day. The waterfall sounded louder, like something was wrong. It pounded instead of trickled. I took a long deep breath.

"You okay?" Amme asked.

"I need to stretch."

I did a downward dog in the grass and Amme placed her hands in front of mine and walked her feet up my ribs until they rested on my low back. We stacked like a human house of cards. She pressed her feet into my sacrum. Blood rushed down to my head and I felt relief. Through my legs, I noticed a crowd of strangers standing around us eating their salads and drinking their teas. Amme lifted her right leg into the sky. With a gentle push off my spine, she kicked her left foot to meet her right. I sat back on my knees and watched her. Amme held that handstand forever.

MY COLLECTION

When Mo was diagnosed with breast cancer and she started losing her hair, I bought my first wig. She and I went to the Lemmon Wig Shop right over there on South Congress. And I remember being impressed by the quality and selection. They looked like real human hair! They were more expensive than what I'd budgeted for, but the sky was the limit for Mo. It was important that she walked out of Lemmon's feeling pretty, or at the very least, amused. I was nervous when we walked in—seeing all those wigs in the window on those cartoon mannequin faces was a little creepy, but the people behind the counter gave us big smiles and encouraged us to try on every wig in the store. Hours later, we rolled out of there with four wigs each, fake eyelashes, and bedazzled press-on nails.

My George had been dead for three months when I found my grown-ass son, Jonathan, in my walk-in closet. I'd heard a wig rustling off one of the six Styrofoam heads. What was he doing in there? Trying one on? My knees trembled and my heart galloped thinking of him finding my collection: a waist-length platinum job, a short red number with bangs, some curly brown locks, a Dolly Parton, a Crystal Gail, and Britney's pink alter ego. I don't know what came over me!—I shouted, *Haven't you taken enough?*

I almost expected my son to come out with Virginia on his head, my long platinum beauty that flipped up at the bottom, because that's just the kind of relationship we had. We were able to joke about the gravest things, but he walked out empty-headed. He looked stunned, pale. Blue eyes glazed over. He couldn't even look at me. His own mother who had bailed him out of jail. Twice. Get out, I said. Get out this minute.

That look he gave me! I can still see it now: his face rippled with repulsion. Who was he to judge me? I didn't want to keep the wigs in a box anymore. They get all bent out of shape and they're never really the same if you don't treat them properly. Why was he on my side of the house anyway? Can't a 56-year-old woman have some privacy? Haven't I suffered enough? Two dead husbands and a troubled son. Most women my age have grandchildren. I've never put any pressure on him.

Now I know it must have been hard, losing his father in the middle of the night. I can still remember when the police knocked on the door. Said those words: car, tree, under-the-influence. A woman passenger—survived without a scratch.

That couldn't be my husband! I remember saying that over and over. There had to be some kind of mistake. The police officer kept repeating my husband's name. He finally had to wrap my fingers around his driver's license. And when I saw his picture, I started crying. I suppose I was screaming. Now that I'm thinking about it, you could've called me hysterical. When Jonathan walked into the living room, I guess I should have composed myself. A six-year-old boy shouldn't see his mother in that state. He shouldn't have had to figure things out by himself. But how was I supposed to control the uncontrollable?

When Sam comes over in the middle of the night, I don't think Jonathan can hear us. I moved my bedroom to the other side of the house next to the pool. I had to. We couldn't afford the hotels anymore. Even the cheap ones add up. Plus, neither of us liked checking in at the front desk. Austin is big, but it's also a small town and I've gotten a little vocal these days. I don't know what has gotten into me. I've never really understood sex before, just went through the motions hoping it would be over soon. It must be those wigs. They make me want to scream. The silky hair that hangs down my back and covers my breasts. Even the short ones that tuck under my ear, they make me feel so giddy. I finally know what this body is for. I don't even mind being older. With my wig, I'm just pretty hair.

Last week when Sam was over, he picked up a picture of Jonathan and said, Right off the bat, I could tell he was yours.

He may have gotten my cheekbones and my almond-shaped eyes, I replied, but he's all his father. He tans like me though. In the summer, we're the same shade. See his glossy eyes? Always looks like he's just been stung by a bee.

Like the time he was playing in the backyard by the black-eyed susans. He used to pick up those daisy-like things and run in circles. The golden flowers matched his straw hair. I remember seeing the yellow jacket flying around his head and instead of crashing onto his shoulder, it landed in the dark center of the flower. He'd reached for butterflies before, orange and red ones, so why would this be any different? From the poolside chairs, Mo and I watched him grab for the yellow and black stripes. I saw the bee land on the webbing between his thumb and index finger. I watched the pain travel up his tan little arm, to his clenched jaw, and just when he was about to wail, we locked eyes, and instead of screaming, he just held it in. Spent his whole life holding it in.

I've never told anyone this before, but the night Jonathan's father died, the police officer asked me if I wanted to know the name of the woman who was in the car. I remember shaking my head. Beating my hands on the policeman's chest. The police officer trying to calm me down. I said, no thank you! But it was printed in the paper the very next day. I didn't know that name. Had no intention of ever looking it up. I did keep those clippings in an album and when Jonathan got older I let him see those scrapbooks. I watched his face when he read about the woman. Saw him wondering who she was, and how strange that someone had been next to him when he died, and it wasn't either of us. But he never did ask, so I never said anything about it. Figured it was all there in black and white.

Jonathan's missing now. It's been a little over a week since he found my collection. Sometimes I wonder what I could have done differently. And all I can come up with is that I did the best I could. If Mo was still with us, I would call her. She'd know what to do. After the accident, Mo drove Jonathan to school on the days I couldn't get up. I know she's watching over him right now, keeping him safe, telling him to do the right thing and come back home to his mama. I don't want to burden Sam with all this. He has his own kids and a sick wife. All I can do is sit here and smoke cigarettes until either the police come knocking again or he walks through that door. Speaking of doors, I locked the closet door. None of that matters anymore. Silly wigs. Making me feel joy—like a girl again.

THE TASTING MENU

Kevin had sunburned his face walking around Fisherman's Wharf, and as soon as he was seated at Le Colonial, he asked a busboy to bring him a rag with ice. He held the compress against his cheek and hung his baldhead out the rattan shuttered window while his wife complained about her interview at McKinsey & Company.

"In the first 30 seconds, a pen exploded in my hands," Lucy said. "I thought it was a minimal disaster until afterwards, when I went to the bathroom and saw that the ink had smeared all over my lips and face. I'm such an idiot! I wondered why he was looking at me so strangely. This trip has been a total waste." Then she coughed and looked at her husband's cheap blue fleece with red embroidered SF BAY on it and said, "I don't understand why you bought that thing."

"It was baltic in the shade," he replied with his brummie British accent.

"Can you take that ridiculous thing off before Mae arrives? You dress smart when we're with your friends. First impressions are important."

"Why do you have to impress her?"

"I don't! It's just...she's a fashion designer and you're wearing a sidewalk fleece!"

"You said that she dressed like a bum in college."

"We all dressed that way. It was grunge. Mae is a good friend. Please?"

"If she's such a good friend, why wasn't she at our wedding?"

"Just take it off."

It was too late. Lucy saw the slight figure walking towards them. She did not recognize Mae from the college memory she had of her: a girl in overalls with kind eyes that swallowed secrets. The only way she identified this person was from Instagram. Lucy had thumbed through hundreds of Mae's photos—in different burlesque costumes, holding hands with drag queens, and being carried off stages by shirtless boys—while Lucy studied for her night classes in her cubicle. It was her cinched waist that she noticed first. Do people in San Francisco wear corsets? She looked like a Shrinky Dink version of her former self. The person Lucy knew ate Cool Ranch Doritos for lunch, Mini-Wheats for dinner, and two bean burritos from the Taco Bell drive-thru at 3:30 am. This person looked like Edith Wharton's Lily Bart right before she keeled over. What would they talk about?

"Lulu," Mae said, stretching out her arms to hug her.

"Ryyyyydes," Lucy replied, unnaturally elongating the vowels. Now it seemed weird calling this woman a silly nickname. She was now Mae Ryder: the brand. Lucy displayed her loyalty by lifting up her baggy sweater and pointing to her low-rise jeans.

"It's so good to finally see you," Mae said, hugging Lucy. "It's been years." Mae turned to Kevin, who removed the ice from his forehead and stood up. He reached across the table to shake Mae's hand, but she leaned forward, kissed both of his cheeks, and said, "*Lovely* to meet you."

"Have you been here long?" Mae noticed a small blister forming on the tip of Kevin's nose.

"Long enough that we should have a drink by now," Kevin lifted his arm as a young woman walked by, "but we can't find a bloody waitress."

Mae waved to the waiter, who signaled that he'd be over after he delivered his tray of umbrella drinks, and apologized to Kevin and Lucy for making one final text. "The new washes are shipping today and I have to approve the final specs."

"Go on," Kevin said.

"You must be so busy," Lucy replied, "running a company and all."

When Mae finished her text, the waiter returned, and without consulting the others she said, "A round of mojitos for the table, please."

Kevin grimaced. "Actually, I'll have a…"

"Just try one," Lucy interrupted.

"It's the house specialty," Mae said. "If you don't like it, we can get something else."

Kevin wanted a pint of beer and some chips. His face hurt like hell and he didn't want a sugary cocktail and infused nibbles, but he knew Lucy would be at him for not trying with her friend, so he obliged. When the leafy drinks arrived, he discarded the straw and took a sip before Mae could make a toast, "Congratulations!" She lifted her glass.

"For what?" Lucy said.

"On your marriage," Mae replied.

"That was ages ago." Lucy watched Kevin gulp down his cocktail. "Now all he has to do is pass the bar." She spoke to Mae as if he wasn't there. "Us both being in school has been extremely stressful on our relationship. At least my company is paying for my MBA, but we still have to deal with Kevin's loans. I'm interviewing in three different states; he can't study for the bar until I get a job."

Mae smiled nervously at Kevin, who reclaimed his straw and started chipping the ice with it. "Consider it a vacation," Mae said.

"That's what I've been trying to tell him," Lucy replied. "But he feels like his life is on hold. Everyone already has a house and we're looking at cheap apartments to rent. But look at you, this big jean designer. I don't even remember you flipping through a magazine. Weren't you a psychology major?"

"Architectural History with a minor in English Literature." Mae put her hands behind her back and tightened the bow on her corset. She wondered how much Lucy had read. Some articles portrayed her as a model-turned-designer, while others accused her of stealing ideas from the man she worked with for three years, sleeping with his business partner, and breaking their team apart.

"So when did you get into fashion?"

Mae took a breath—she'd told this story to so many reporters she had it down to a science. "After I went to Parsons, I still didn't know what I wanted to do except move to San Francisco. When I got here, I answered an ad on Craigslist to be a fit model at Levi's."

"Don't they have mannequins for that," Kevin said, curtly.

"Exactly," Mae said, sincerely. "I thought I'd be a mannequin with brains, offering feedback about different styles. When the head designer from Levi's started another company I went with him. I had more ideas than he did. So I created my own prototype using a cashmere blend, and it all just sort of happened."

"That's when this whole persona thing started," Lucy said, then backtracked, "I mean, retro-look."

Mae took another breath and changed the subject to something they still had in common. "And how is Laura doing?"

"She's gone off the deep end," Lucy replied. "I almost blocked her on Facebook."

"What?" Mae couldn't imagine Laura doing anything wrong.

"Don't you see her posts?"

"To be honest, my intern does all my social media. I stopped everything. It was too distracting. Hours would go by and I wondered where I'd been."

"I don't look at Facebook that much either," Lucy insisted, "but she has become..."

"A pro-life activist," Kevin interjected.

"Laura?" Mae shook her head. "Not shocking. You remember how religious she was. She went to church every Sunday. The time she visited me here, she brought home the bulletin and left it on my dresser with the times circled."

"You would think she'd know the statistics," Lucy looked into Mae's caramel eyes. "One out of four women have had an abortion. There were four of us that lived together senior year."

Mae, not knowing how much Kevin knew, said, "Yeah, you would think."

Mae remembered that day clearly. Lucy in a hospital gown. Mae, sitting in the waiting room with the mothers waiting for their teenage daughters. Mae remembered the conversation she had with one of the mothers; they spoke about succulents. There was a pearly lavender flower, Mae had never seen such fleshy leaves, she wanted to squeeze the petals with her thumb and index finger. "It's an Echeveria," the mother said. Then she told me to use sand in the soil when you plant them. If potting, pour the sand on top. The only way you can kill a succulent is by giving it too much water.

Mae remembered the waiting room, that it smelled like vanilla formaldehyde. She would always associate that smell with the distant look on Lucy's face when she walked down the hall with her jeans unbuttoned and an oversized sweater, very similar to the outfit she had on at dinner. The feeling of helplessness she felt when she put her arm around Lucy, walked her around the car, and opened the passenger door.

"We're staying with Laura next weekend," Lucy said.

"I thought you just said you almost blocked her on Facebook?"

"I have another interview in Chicago."

Mae scratched her head.

"Thank you for letting us stay with you!" Lucy sensed Mae's distance. "And warning us about the key. It did stick, but we figured it out."

"Good," Mae said. "I had my assistant on call in case you needed to get in."

"Can we order?" asked Kevin. "They haven't even brought us menus yet."

"I should have told you," Mae replied. "I ordered us the tasting menu. My treat."

"Fantastic," Kevin said, obviously unenthused.

When the food arrived, they used long red chopsticks to eat small portions of grilled lemongrass filet mignon, shredded green papaya prawns, and jasmine rice with curry. This would not fill him up, and he already planned on getting a late night slice. As the two women played catch-up, Kevin's eyes traced the oriental rugs, the bamboo ceiling fans, and the patchwork tile floors. He stared at a black-and-white photo of a young Vietnamese man with round-rimmed glasses. He remembered an article he'd read at Cambridge by the Vietnamese revolutionary,

Ngô Văn, who struggled against the colonialism that this restaurant capitalized on. Kevin thought about Văn's arrests, being tortured and imprisoned with breaks of freedom. He didn't think marriage would be this unbearable. He thought that he could do all the formalities as long as he had such breaks of freedom. He wondered if the newly rich Mae Ryder had heard of Ngô Văn. He despised the fact that Americans could become rich without knowing a thing about history, while he owed a hundred grand to a government that wasn't even his. When Lucy excused herself to the bathroom, he asked her about Ngô Văn.

"What?" Mae said.

"The picture, behind you."

Mae turned around, studied the photo, and said, "Could be." Like she knew whom he was referring to, then, flipped her hair and said, "My favorite restaurant in London is this little place on Brewer Street called Randall and Aubin. Have you been? There's always a line out the door for their rotisserie chicken. It's right in Soho."

"What is the part of town that's similar to Soho here?" He replied. "The Caster?"

"The Castro." Mae enunciated the "o."

He still could not understand her. "Could you spell it?"

"C-a-s-t-r-o."

"I'd like to check it out."

"To go dancing? Clubbing here isn't as good as London or Berlin."

"I'm more of a pub guy," he said.

When Lucy returned, the ice had melted in Kevin's rag. He opened it up and covered his entire face and balding head.

"I think I might walk downstairs," Kevin said.

"She hasn't even asked for the check yet," Lucy replied. "You can stay and say thank you." Then to Mae, "We can't even afford a meal like this and he's being rude."

"No," Mae said. "Please! Go downstairs. Get some air. I'll get the check."

"We were talking about going somewhere else," Kevin smiled at Mae, and she thought she'd ill-judged him. He wasn't rude. She'd just picked the wrong spot.

"Yeah," Mae said. "I have the perfect place."

Mae took them to a neighborhood bar with loud music, uneven bar stools, and sticky tables. A bar like they would've gone to in college with televisions flickering sports and boys wearing backwards baseball hats as they pointed and sighed at the flat screens. They took a seat next to the jukebox and as soon as Kevin went to the bar, Lucy started talking about an email relationship she'd been having with one of her co-workers. He told her all the time that he liked her hair and how funny she was in the 10:00am meeting. Lucy fidgeted with her sweater as she spoke, and Mae's eyes naturally gazed down. "I've gained weight," Lucy said. "You've gotten so thin. Everyone in this state is so Goddamn thin."

"You look great," Mae said. "Are you still talking to this guy from work?"

"No, I broke it off. It was just nice having some attention."

"Doesn't Kevin give you any?"

They looked at Kevin, who was at the bar looking at the game on television. "What do you think?"

Mae wanted to ask, Why did you marry him? But refrained.

Lucy started chatting with the guys at the next table. They joked around with her but kept glancing at Mae, who gave them a polite smile. Mae looked at her watch. It was only 9:00pm. She wondered how much longer she would have to stay. When would it be polite enough to go home? Lucy started touching the guy's arms while she looked at Kevin, the guy looked at Mae for help, unfazed Kevin looked at the bartender and ordered a shot. The awkwardness of it all compelled Mae to sit next to Kevin and down her first shot since college. Then her second.

The tequila made her silly. She high-fived Kevin when the rest of the bar cheered. She swayed on the stool to the pounding drums. Everyone suddenly appeared to be at the same level of intoxication. Instead of bumping into each other, the people bounced off each other, clearing the path for the person carrying the most drinks. The female bartender, or perhaps just a random girl in a tank top, hopped on the bar and started pouring liquor straight into people's mouths *Coyote Ugly*-style. Mae surprised herself by opening her mouth. All bets were off. The jukebox played Guns N' Roses and Neil Diamond but when Biggie Smalls started playing, Mae felt the bass in her ribcage. Lucy ran over to find her and pulled her on the makeshift dance floor.

Everyone in the bar knew the chorus, but Mae and Lucy knew the entire song. When "Hypnotize" came out at Clemson University, it had been life changing for them both. Before that, they only listened to jam bands and would sit around and get stoned and eat boxes of cereal. This song got them off the couch. It made them feel urban in their provincial town. A few guys tried to intrude, but they just spat out the words to each other. "I put hoes in N-Y onto D-K-N-Y. Miami, D.C., prefer Versace! All Philly hoes, go with Moschino..." Even in the silly corset, Mae was still the same moon-faced girl. Lucy gave her a hug so tight that they almost fell onto the sticky floor. Mae's body remembered her friend's embrace. It pulled her back to a time when she was the insecure one, and Lucy the more confident.

"Let's go," Kevin tapped Lucy.

Mae nodded. It was time. The evening was over. The three of them walked out of the bar. Mae, sweaty from dancing, pushed open the door and let the cool breeze hit her face. She suddenly wanted a cigarette. She hadn't had one in years. A group of girls got out of a cab and lit one right in front of her.

"I love your corset," one of them screamed.

"Thank you," Mae replied.

"Kevin," Mae shouted, as he made a move toward the empty cab, "My flat is only a few blocks away."

"How far is the Castro?" he asked the driver.

"About two miles."

"Kevin, what are you doing?" Lucy asked. "We're going home."

"I will see you later," he said.

"You don't know the address." Lucy looked confused. "What's The Castro?"

The cab driver looked at his steering wheel.

"Another part of town," Mae said.

Lucy pulled at Kevin's sleeve and spoke firmly in his ear. Mae thought he looked like a statue, clutching the cab door, and she wanted to pull Lucy away.

"I'm going," he finally said.

Mae pulled out a pen and wrote down her address. "You might need this."

"What's in the Castro, Kevin?" Lucy started to raise her voice. "Why would you leave your wife and her friend and go to another part of town? We're going with you!" Lucy pushed him into the cab. "Rydes, get in."

Mae opened the front door and shared a glance with the driver, who made a U-turn on Divisadero. Mae turned the radio up, but this only encouraged Lucy to speak louder.

"He's never done this before, Mae. I don't know why he's insisting on going out alone tonight."

Mae remained silent.

"Why are you acting so strange in front of my friend?"

Breaks of freedom, he thought. He could do all formalities with breaks of freedom.

"He's never done this before," Lucy kept repeating herself.

"There's another bar on Divis," Mae suggested. "It's halfway between my house and the Castro. Why don't we stop for a drink and if it's lame we can catch another cab over the hill? Kevin, is that okay with you?"

"I'm sure you only want to go to another bar," Lucy said.

"Fine," he said.

"Madrone," Mae told the driver. "Right there!"

The cab made a screeching stop. Across the street, there was a small line hugging the corner of the bar and four lanes of traffic speeding down Fell Street. Mae paid for the cab as she and Lucy stepped out onto the street. Kevin remained firmly planted. He told the driver to carry on, not looking at either of them. Lucy held onto the door, screaming at him to get out.

"Lulu," Mae said, "let him go."

Lucy slammed the door and ran across the street. Kevin unzipped his SF Bay fleece, and the driver took off up Divisadero Street.

Mae waited at the light as the wind whipped around her bare shoulders causing her to shiver. What she wouldn't do to go home and fast-forward to Sunday night. Instead she went inside the loud bar, ordered two dirty martinis, and finally asked Lucy the obvious question.

"Because we wanted the same thing," Lucy said, "a family." Lucy paused, but then continued, "Did you really sleep with your boss?"

"It was more complicated than that."

"It always is."

"I was tired of being a body for hire," Mae paused. "I was not made for only one purpose."

"None of us are," Lucy said matter-of-factly, and they clinked glasses as if they were talking about the same thing.

The next morning, Mae pulled the pillow over her head, ill. She had no idea what time it was, but she hoped for afternoon. Light infused the room, warming her body. She kicked the covers off and was planning to sneak out for coffee and bagels, when she heard a knock on the door. "Come in."

Kevin entered the room, his face peeling, head down. "Lucy wanted me to apologize for my behavior last night."

"No worries, Kevin. We were all pretty drunk."

Lucy suddenly appeared behind him and pushed him closer to the bed.

"Do you know he was already home by the time we got in?" Lucy insisted.

"I hardly remember coming home," Mae lied and pushed her messy hair out of her face. "I was thinking about getting bagels. Do you have any requests?"

"Did you tell her you're not gay?" Lucy asked.

"What?" Mae couldn't believe what was happening. "You don't have to tell me anything." She swung her legs to the floor.

"It's so funny," Lucy looked at Kevin. "I told you she would think you were gay."

"I'm not gay," Kevin said sincerely. "I just wanted to get a drink and I wanted to be alone. No offense."

"None taken," Mae replied.

"I went into one of those bars, ordered a drink, and came here."

"He was already home by the time we got in," Lucy repeated.

"Do you like sweet bagels?" Mae kicked around for her ballet flats. "Because I prefer stinky ones like onion and garlic. But I only eat them if someone else joins me."

"Poppy. I like poppy," Kevin said.

Lucy looked at Mae, who appeared younger, makeup-less and disheveled. "That's it!" Lucy pointed to Mae's nightstand. "You were wearing false eyelashes. I couldn't quite place it. Do you wear those fake things every day?"

"Not every day." Mae peeled them off her nightstand and threw them in the trash. Then to Kevin, "Sesame? I mean Poppy."

As soon as Mae shut the front door, Lucy picked up a picture of Mae on the mantle, next to a fleshy succulent plant.

"Do you believe how much effort she puts into her appearance?"

"If you'd ask me, she looks like a drag queen," Kevin said.

"Did you see that pillbox hat she put on before she left?"

"I know. As if the paparazzi is waiting outside for her."

"I'd rather be fat," Lucy said with a laugh.

"Darling, you're perfect."

NEW LOW

The night of my stepfather's funeral I drank openly with my mom. We sat by the pool, listening to the crescendo of crickets. The wind chimes made out of coffee mugs, forks, and plates rattled in the occasional breeze. She lifted the top of the cooler, dug her hand in the ice, and said, "You might as well have one with me, Jon. I know what you've been hiding in your room." It was the first time we drank together since rehab, then jail.

"He kept his cards close to his vest," she continued. "He could've had a pair of aces or the hammer. I never would've known." She brushed her new black bangs over her forehead.

It felt like she wanted to tell me something, something I didn't want to hear. There are some things you don't want to know about your mother.

"You know George and I hadn't been physical for many, many years," she said.

I kept my eyes on the pool. For as long as I could remember, George and my mother had slept in separate bedrooms. This had always embarrassed me. Everyone else's parents shared a bedroom. I didn't want my friends to know that my house was different than theirs. So, I told them George watched TV in the den and sometimes he fell asleep in there.

"Would you be okay if I dated someone again?"

I thought this was strange because George's body was still warm, but I said, "Are you talking about dating or getting some ass, because there are apps for that now."

"Oh, I've already downloaded Geezer," she replied.

We laughed. It felt good. It made me feel like things might be okay.

"I can't thank you enough for taking care of George," she said. "I couldn't handle seeing him so feeble. I just couldn't face it. He reminded me how little time I have left in this bag of flesh."

"I'm pretty sure I owe you one," I said, folding my napkin. Remembering the guard in jail, telling me to re-do the military corners, then fold the extra blanket at the foot of the bed, and place the folding chair on top of the bed so he could inspect the walls. No cobwebs allowed. Cobwebs were as dangerous as leaving a nudie picture of your girlfriend out (and Maria had sent several). When I finally got it right, I felt a sense of accomplishment.

"I had to identify your father's body," mom said, pulling me further back in time. Back then, every day of my life has been a rerun of the past. George's death was sure to bring up the Disappointment Highlight Reel. I'd never heard this one before.

"...seeing him on the table like that...still looking like him...not twisted or bloody...but handsome...and just as far away as ever...the image never left me."

I listened to the crickets. After a while, you just forget about them. The screeching became part of the air. I let the sound pulse with my heartbeat until I merged with the sound. I closed my eyes and tried to stay there as long as possible. When my eyes blinked open, I drank my beer and lit a cigarette. I imagined my body as a vast garbage dump and I inhaled. I planned to drink until my liver and kidneys pickled.

"I shouldn't have told you that."

"It's alright," I said.

"It's just hard for me to keep things from you."

I nodded and looked at the bottom of the pool.

In minimum-security prison, most people were quiet about their crimes. I let people wonder about mine as I wondered about theirs. Often, I was disappointed when I found out about their embezzlement schemes, pawnshop frauds, or holding up a liquor store with a toy gun. They weren't real criminals. They were just sad sacks plagued with the same manipulation magnet as me. I wondered if these magnets, like vaccines, were given at birth? Or was it a degenerate trait passed down by our ancestors? Or did something traumatic need to happen to you as a child to have such luck?

Some of the guys had big personalities. They were charmers. Curley's eyes lit up every time he talked about his Ponzi scheme. You wanted to believe him. Join his dream. Hijack his heist. It took skills to lie and cheat, to deceive the people closest to you. You do it partially because it's fun to see what you can get away with and partially because you have no control over it. Before my second DWI, I fake-worked for three months. Instead of going to the Odd Duck to wait tables, I went straight to the bar and hung out with the other regulars who lived their lives in hiding. These folks had either accomplished their dreams and became disillusioned by them or, like me, never had any at all. They were there from 10am to 4pm, drinking Bloody Marys, Jamesons on the rocks, and Mexican beers. I drank whiskey neat.

Most days, I sat next to a guy named Kevin. He claimed to be a retired corporate lawyer, mentioned law school now and then, seemed more liberal than most people from Austin, and his nose always ran with clear snot. I got the feeling that this was what he wanted to do more than sitting with his kids, being on vacation with his wife, or being in a courtroom. I didn't blame him. It was nice to be in a place where people didn't know your failures or have any expectations of you. You could just be yourself.

"How many more days until Spring Training?"

"127," Kevin replied. "I think the Rangers got a chance this year."

"You going again?"

"That's the plan."

I pointed my finger to the bartender, Max. He was a concert cellist who now played bass in a couple Austin punk bands. He slid me a Jameson.

"Do you know how to recruit a terrorist?" Kevin clinked my glass.

"How?" I held my drink, waiting for the punchline.

"Make him think his life has purpose."

We hit our glasses.

The day after George's funeral was another scorcher: 103 degrees. Although we no longer dated, Maria asked me to her friend's barbeque. She walked over to my house holding a fruit salad, looking very tan, and wearing a short cotton dress over her bathing suit.

"Have you ever tried a fruit salad with kiwi?"

I didn't think I had. The green color popped out of the red and blue.

"You watch," she said, "it'll be the first thing to go."

She handed me the salad, and I gave her my mom's car keys. I still had a suspended license and couldn't drive. As she hopped into the driver's seat, one of her dress straps fell off her shoulder while the pink swimsuit hugged her neck. "What?" She slammed the door.

"Nothing." I placed the strap of her dress back on her shoulder.

"Now that we broke up, you start noticing me? Typical."

"Maybe you should've worn neon more often."

"Asshole." She smiled.

When she pressed down the clutch and shifted the gear into reverse, the car jerked and the fruit spilled all over.

"Shit," she said, putting the car in gear.

I opened the glove compartment for some napkins, but only found a piece of notebook paper. I read the note before I attempted to clean up the mess.

"Hurry up," Maria said. "It's staining my dress."

I grabbed an old T-shirt from the backseat and tossed it to her. My other hand still held the note. Just then, my mom walked out, smiling and waving; she probably wondered what we were doing sitting in the driveway until she saw the piece of paper in my hand.

"Drive," I shouted to Maria as I watched my mother's face grow concerned.

"Do you mind telling me what's going on?" Maria reversed.

I handed her the note.

"Who's Sammy?"

"I have no idea. Never heard his name before."

"How do you know it's a guy? I'm sorry, but...'Love, Your Favorite Licking Machine'—that sounds like a woman."

"I might get sick."

"You'd think she would keep the note in her room or something."

"Yeah," I said. "You would think."

The next day I sold some of George's opiates to a guy at the Odd Duck and bought ten cases of beer. In the evenings, I could hear my mom picking up the empty cans that overflowed on the garage floor. I never did say anything to her. And she never said anything about my drinking, but she knew that I knew: I took care of her dying husband while she got licked by this Sammy-person. I wondered if she even got that promotion? I thought about all the nights she had to "work late," when she stayed at the motel across the way because the 45-minute commute was too hard with her "night blindness."

To deceive, you had to be consistent. Had to remember your schedule. Put your uniform on. Leave with a false urgency, say things like, *Shit, my manager is going to kill me*, so your mom would give you encouragement as you hustled out the door, pinning your name tag on your pocket and telling you to tuck in your shirt. Blocks away, the effort drained from your face and your real self emerged.

Eventually, I gave George's La-Z-Boy to Goodwill and put a desk where the hospital bed used to be. No one used the desk but the den felt empty without it. My mother started dressing differently, wearing long cotton skirts instead of pants, turquoise jewelry hung from her ears. She moved into the guest bedroom with a sliding glass door leading to the pool. We didn't talk anymore. We barely looked at each other.

Weeks later, when I finished the cases of beer, I was back to my old ways, rummaging around the house. I found myself in her bedroom, skimming through her drawers for some cash. When I flicked on her closet light, I thought I'd fallen into a black hole. I closed my eyes. When I opened them, I thought I was transported to a Vegas dressing room. Various colored lingerie filled the walls. There was a vanity table and chair with lights around the mirror and a hanging rack with nylons and feather boas. I wondered if my mother had rented it out to a local dancer. When I looked up and saw the Styrofoam heads with wigs, I almost fainted. I had to touch it, to believe it. I reached for one of the heads and pulled down a wig when I heard—

"What in the world?" she gasped. "Get out! Get out of here this instant! And stay out. Not just out of my room, but out of this house. I mean it. I want you out!"

The long red wig felt silkier than it looked. I threw it at her and said, "Gladly."

For a week I slept on a cement plank behind a Whole Foods, an oak tree shading me from the 90-degree sun. I rested my head on my backpack and rubbed my sweaty face with my dirty palms. My beard had grown beyond a shadow and moved into full stubble. I looked down at my jeans. They were ripped, but I had worn ripped jeans before. I was dirty, but I still looked like a kid who could have been camping, not a 28-year-old man who hadn't showered in days.

As I walked around to the front of the Whole Foods, I felt the heat on the pavement through my worn down shoes. It was lunchtime, and the parking lot was filled with mini-vans. Kids were being pushed in carts with green balloons tied around their wrists. My arm was in the trash can, elbow deep, rummaging for a half-eaten brown box of food when I saw Scarlett. She was wearing a beige linen suit with nude high heels and was drinking a Jamba Juice. Her auburn hair was lighter or maybe straighter than I remembered—but it was *her*. I pulled my arm out of the can like I was going to walk up and give her a hug. Her face winced the moment she saw me.

"Scarlett," I yelled, but she just kept walking. "It's me," I said. "I was camping. I dropped my wallet in here by mistake."

She turned around. When her eyes caught mine, I felt incredibly big and incredibly small.

"Jonathan?" she asked, staying a good distance away. "What are you doing?" She paused, "Sorry to hear about George. My mom told me he passed."

"Thank you." I put my hands in my pockets and looked at her shoes. "You look amazing. I saw that you got married. Nashville, right?"

"Yeah, just home visiting my parents."

"Still teaching?"

"Tenth grade at an all girls private school."

"That's good."

"What about you? Still living with your mom?"

"Not exactly. I've been kinda camping out back trying to figure things out."

She interrogated me with her eyes and I remembered all the fights we'd had, her throwing things at me, me pinning her down on the bed, us crying and holding each other.

"You still drawing?" she asked." "I still have one of your comic books that you and Zach made."

"He's in LA now," I said, like we still kept in touch.

"Yeah, I heard."

She kept leaning on her toes as if she planned to flee. My eyes begged her to stay. I tried to remember anyone's name from college or who they married—just to keep talking to her for a moment longer—but my mind went blank.

"I hope you figure things out, Jon." She looked deep into my eyes and for a moment everything went away: my dirty hands, my ripped jeans, the screaming kids, the slamming trunks, and it was just me and her. Then she tilted her head and sucked on her blueberry smoothie like she'd been right about me all along.

"Good to see you," she said.

"Yeah. You, too."

I guess she changed her mind about grocery shopping. She ran to her car. Her legs, endless in those flesh-colored heels. Then I had that black hole sensation again, like gravity was pulling me down so much that everything went dark. They say that happens when a star dies. Maybe we had all these stars inside us and they're dying all the time but we just don't notice? When I opened my eyes, I knew what I'd become. And just like I didn't know how I got there, I will never know how or why I changed after. Do we ever know the stripped-down acts of the will or the antecedent order of anything? All I know is that I started by making my bed like it was the most important thing in the world. I started living like a terrorist, like my life had purpose.

CHEAP HOTEL

It's three o'clock in the morning, and tomorrow's marathon swells the city so much that all of our regular haunts were booked.

Bed bugs, I think, looking at the sheets.

"Tanya, are you alright?" Jeff asks while unbuttoning his collar.

"I'm not feeling well," I lie. "Do you mind if we just hold each other?"

I can tell he minds, but it is late. And honestly, what can he do? Complain? He already has a wife he argues with; he has to be forgiving with me. He undresses, lies down, and pats the empty side of the bed.

Through the walls, I hear coughs and sneezes, but I think: pertussis. The rough sheets irritate my sensitive skin. Outside, a woman yells jumbled profanities and I wonder if someone has stolen her purse or if it's a nightly routine. It seems to go on for hours, while Jeff snores lightly with a pillow between his knees. Hours later, I rummage through my purse for a Xanax.

When I fumble back into bed, I wrap myself around Jeff and smell the sheets. They are odorless, just like the nicer hotels that have never made me feel this way. I think about Jeff's wife, his children. I wonder if there is a hidden camera and it's streaming live to the nurses huddled around the front desk at the hospital, watching us cling to each other.

"I called it," Rhonda will rejoice as she turns to go check her patient's pulse. "She wasn't ready to assist."

"It's always the one you least suspect," Christine will say to bitchy Ken, then close her clipboard. "She looks like she could be his daughter."

"Boring," Ken will scoff as he swivels in his chair. "I'd rather be watching a cat ride a rhino. Have you seen it? I've watched it nonstop."

The Xanax hushes their voices and my body relaxes. The thought of people watching me, watching us, causes my hips to stir. I press myself behind Jeff, like he usually presses behind me, and awaken him with my hands. I climb on top of him. His eyes remain closed, but his neck rolls from right to left with a vague smile. He wants to stay in this dream-like state, and I become the fantasy behind his lids. But it's the man, maybe the woman, behind the peephole whom I'm moving for. She likes the arch of my back, the circular motion of my hips. Jeff lifts his hands to my breasts and squeezes my nipples with just the right amount of pressure, and I scream louder than the woman outside my window.

But what if there isn't a camera, and invisible mites are not burrowing into my skin. What if this goes on for years without anyone knowing anything. Does that make it a relationship? Will the house-keeper, who stopped my heart when she knocked on the door, come into the room and throw away our secrets? Wash the sheets and mingle our needs with everyone else's?

Tomorrow we will put on our scrubs and wash our hands clean. Jeff will call his wife, tell her he'd fallen asleep at the hospital again. He will say, "Good morning," to his sons and it will be like nothing happened. I will take an Adderall and meet with my patients, who will lie to me about the drugs they have taken, and I will look at them knowingly. At least one of them will ask, "Are you even old enough to be a doctor?" And I will hardly recognize my own voice when I say, "Yes."

DON'T FEED THE PIGEONS

"Are they even 21?" I ask.

"Babies," Michelle says. "We could be their mothers."

I look at Heath. I'm guessing he's forty, a couple of years older than me, but he just looks down at his checkerboard high-tops. Like an aging beauty queen, he ignores the topic of age. He feels and looks boyish. The few times I've been here, I've seen him leave with a different lady each night.

"I will never work another Saturday night," Michelle says. "I make as much on a Wednesday. If I wanted to work with ungrateful children, I would've been a kindergarten teacher. I have to go back in there."

Michelle stands up and throws her arms around Todd, the large bouncer with a baritone voice who graces the stage with his seven-piece soul band on the nights he's not working the door. Todd hasn't left his stool since I snagged one of the four tables outside. With his left hand, he halts the flow of traffic coming in and out of the half-door so Michelle can easily slide behind the bar.

I came here alone because I knew Michelle was working and Heath helped himself to the seat across from me. I met Michelle six months ago in a writing class, and we bonded over Grace Paley's "Wants." That plumber snake metaphor. *Hello, my life!* Perhaps, we both wanted to be a different type of person. The kind who got paid for making art instead of serving others. I instantly gravitated to Michelle's poetry, and after months of being paired together in class, she invited me to one of her rock shows.

When I entered the sweaty concert, Michelle was on stage with her band. Her whisper-voice sounded like walking through a forest barefoot. The room fell quiet enough to hear the branches breaking under her feet. Her songs vacillated between hopelessness and being hopeful, wanting love and needing space, being rejected and rejecting others. They became my soundtrack when I cleaned the house and drove the kids to school.

"Emma, how many kids do you have?" Heath blurts out.

"Three."

"That's what I heard." His finger taps his upper lip. "That's incredible. I'm impressed you're still out."

I know it must seem strange to some people that I'm "still out," but coming from Heath it hurts. You would think he would understand my restlessness. The need to feel like a person, to talk about things other than my children's schedules. It felt nice to be amongst artists.

"I'm human," I say in a heavy and embarrassing tone. So I try to lighten it. "And I like the night." I take a drag from my cigarette and look up at the fingernail moon. "I miss being out at night. What? You have one and you're still out."

"But three? In San Francisco. You must be rich."

I narrow my eyes and look through the window. I observe Michelle, the other bartender, and a bar-back pace, spin, and dance around each other until 2:00 am. They twist off splits of Prosecco, unscrew cheap bottles of wine, shake hundreds of margaritas, and pour countless beers from the taps. It looks like a party. Michelle's close friends huddle around the well, lapping up the free drinks and telling jokes, looking for the nightly conquest or at the very least, tomorrow's social media banter to get through the hangover. From where I'm sitting, it feels like life itself.

"When's your next show?" I ask.

"Next month at The Independent. You and Michelle should come."

"I will if I can."

I almost say, I've seen you play at the Great American and at The Paramount in Oakland, but I don't. It's strange meeting someone after you've heard their songs. It feels unfair, even creepy, to listen inside someone's heart, when they don't know a thing about you. Or even stranger to assume that you know something about them because you've heard their music.

"None of the moms in Dylan's school are sexy." He reaches across the table to drink the tequila that Michelle left behind and pulls out one of my cigarettes.

"You check out moms at Dylan's school?"

"Well, I'm single now."

"I'm just surprised that you're looking at moms instead of meeting women after one of your shows."

"I want to meet a woman with kids," he says. "You know, they get it."

I look away and wonder what they get. That they already have kids so they won't want one from you? That they receive daily love and affection so they aren't as needy? Yet, they're still dissatisfied so that's where you swoop in.

"You just don't seem like the other moms. I didn't even know you had kids. Most moms, all they talk about is their kids. You're tight-lipped about it."

"Maybe that's a bad thing."

"I don't think so. I volunteer a lot at the school and I was hoping to make friends with the other parents. Most of the people that volunteer are mothers and all they seem to do is gossip about each other and the other kids."

"I just keep my sunglasses on."

"Me, too. Want to hear something sad?"

"Not really."

"It's really sad."

"Don't tell me."

"The only other mother who was like me, well, like us. She wore sunglasses, too. Then a scarf with her sunglasses. One of the other mothers told me she had cancer."

"That is sad," I say.

"No, it gets worse. She died."

"Nothing like talking about cancer while smoking," I say, twisting out my cigarette. "That's terrible. Too sad to think about or I'll have to go home."

"Well, we don't want that." He grins mischievously and exposes his chipped tooth and I find myself smiling into his murky eyes. "I just want to keep on living and making cool shit. Everyone else seems like they're dying, and all they have to live for is their kids. I mean, I love my kid. But I'm not going to stop touring because he's in school. His mom is watching him, he's safe. He wouldn't want me to give up my music just so I can be with him everyday, you know? If you give up your passion, you have nothing to give."

"Exactly," I lift up my drink and Heath clinks it. "I've been trying to make some time for myself, um, for my writing."

"It's important."

A line forms behind us. I twist my neck and look in between the girls in dresses and guys in plaid shirts to the unlit awnings across the street. The crowd has changed a lot since I moved to San Francisco twenty years ago. You don't hear conversations about movies or art anymore. Everyone's talking about rent prices and Google buses and looking at their phones. It's not just the new kids. It's all of us. All of us have changed. I take out my phone and make sure my friend Kim hasn't texted me, telling me one of the kids is up. Heath checks his phone. He spins through Instagram. Liking a few photos, mostly of bands. I can see a couple attractive girls clutching ukuleles and silly cat photos on his screen.

"What about one of these ladies?" I point to a threesome in skinny jeans, heels, and bangs. "You know, I can't tell if people are pretty or just young."

"You're just as vibrant as any of these girls."

I laugh.

"What?"

"Vibrant. It's kind of like saying your grandmother's spry."

"No, it's not."

"Yes, it is."

"Don't underestimate yourself."

"I wasn't underestimating myself. I was talking about them. I guess I want them to know how lovely they are. I had no idea. Now it seems wasteful."

"Well, I hope your husband still tells you that you're beautiful."

"I'm afraid not," I say, my voice getting thin. "Words like that stop after kids. You just see each other differently. The focus changes. You don't dote on each other anymore."

"But it doesn't have to be that way. I still tell my wife, well, now ex-wife, that she's beautiful. She still is. Sexy, too."

"And look how good it turned out." I smile sweetly, but I can tell I've caused some offense.

My eyes jump to the expensive bikes locked up in pairs at each parking meter. Motorcycles rev and pulse, a low rider's bass thumps as it stalls at the yellow light, and a mariachi band warms up until Todd says, "Not tonight. Too packed." They hang their heads and walk down the block. As each hour passes, I start to see the cracks through the window. I notice that Michelle no longer charms the entire bar, rather she deals with impatient people who barely tip or say thank you. I watch Michelle press her earplugs into her ears and lean into the callow faces. Her eyes, angry and elsewhere. Behind me, the people in line talk about how strong the margaritas are here and how they have raised their prices from 7 to 18 dollars overnight.

"It's a lime crisis," one of them says.

It's true, I think. All of these bars are at risk of shutting down. Rents are rising, prices must go up, the locals who've been going here for 20 plus years are forced to go somewhere else. Unless the bartender knows you and gives you the old price. Just then the wind picks up and Michelle walks out the half-door with two tequila gimlets and I smile. She's never been this attentive to me before and I'm grateful not to have to go into the crowded bar. She places the drinks on the table, ties the flannel around her waist, and sits up straight in a black tank top displaying her tiny physique. Michelle is newly blond and has a tattoo of a cherry blossom on her right shoulder. The same tattoo that almost every girl in the Mission has, but I'm quite certain Michelle was the first to get it. She slides me and Heath a drink.

"Just what I needed," I joke.

"If I drink that," Heath says, "I'll be drunk."

"Well, we don't want that." Michelle takes the drink back for herself and begins one of her funny tirades. "If another kid waves me down like it's an emergency and then asks me for water, I might fucking kill somebody. And when did people start saying, 'Can I do?' Instead of, 'May I have?'" She opens her suede purse and pinches tobacco into a rolling paper.

Heath and I laugh as Michelle does her routine about toddlers, techies, and Teslas until a man with a guitar strapped to his back staggers towards us. He has moppy gray hair and wears black women's sunglasses. He doesn't look unlike Keith Richards. At least his clothes are as colorful, his teeth as tobacco stained, and his face as elaborately wrinkled. I wonder if Michelle knows him, like she knows all of the other musicians and panhandlers on this street. I wait for her lead. She acts like he's a ghost. She keeps talking as he stands directly between us, his hands on his hips, and his spine arched like the fingernail moon behind him.

I finally turn to acknowledge him and when I do, I startle with recognition. It's the guy who supposedly broke into Yoko Ono's house. I've walked past him for years while he strummed his guitar with only three strings, singing like he was opening for the Stones. I have some singles in my pocket, but I'm not certain if I should give them to him. I don't work here, but my friends do. Even Heath used to be the doorman here. Working in the service industry in San Francisco, there is an additional job of keeping the homeless away from the patrons.

Michelle raises her normally soft voice and delivers her signature line to the man, "Yer doin' great, pal. Keep walkin." But he doesn't move. Instead, he asks her for something, but I can't hear what it is because Heath is blabbing about himself. The man hovers over Michelle, violating her work break. For a blink, she seems to vacate her body. Almost vanish. I see her disappearing but nobody else does. Just her tough wiry exterior. I want this man to stop bothering her. I want her to be able to sit down, have a laugh, and stop tending to everyone's needs for a Goddamn minute. I assume that he's asking for a cigarette, so I put my hand in the pocket of my purple velvet jacket and place my pack on the table for the taking. But when he turns my way he asks, "How about you, darling? Can I get a kiss?"

His face is so close that I can see my reflection in his bug-like glasses and smell his unwashed body. I glance at Heath who is tapping his foot, then Michelle who is stone-faced, smoking her cigarette. If I thought it would make Michelle's night easier, I'd do it. Because isn't that why I'm sitting outside past midnight, smoking cigarettes with a friend-of-a-friend? But instead, I follow her lead, and I turn my body away from him.

The guy is relentless. He points to his cheek. "Come on," he says, leaning over me.

"Sorry, buddy. You're doin' great," I glance at Michelle. She nods. "Keep walking."

Michelle moves her head like she's teaching me something. And maybe she is.

"Closing should only take me a half-hour," Michelle says to me, "stick around and we can have a nightcap."

"Last call," Todd yells at the people on the street. "All the glasses need to go inside. You two can stay," he says to Heath and me. The lights in the bar turn on, and a sea of people stagger out onto the sidewalk saying hopeless things to each other, desperately trying to find someone (anyone) who will go home with them. How funny that we drink to avoid loneliness yet the only time we're brave enough to ask someone to go home with us is when we can't remember it? I catch Heath's eyes. They are darker than I'm used to, almost flat. Nothing sparkly about them. There's a rehearsed shyness to his stare.

"He already has an ice cream cone," Heath continues his story about his son, "and he's crying because he wants another." He shakes his head in disbelief, zips his coat to his collar, and takes another sip of brown liquor. "He hadn't even had three licks and he's already crying. Then I look like the bad dad telling him to buck up, enjoy the cone you have."

"It's so true," I say. "No matter what you do. They always want more. I've said some pretty terrible things this week to my kids."

"Really?"

"My husband has been traveling a ton and they outnumber me. I'm amazed by what came out of my mouth."

"Like what?"

"Nothing I care to repeat," I smile.

Through the window, I can see Michelle washing a glacier's worth of pint glasses. She looks neither tired nor irritated, simply absorbed in cleaning the glasses. She looks up and waves us in. And although I liked talking to Heath, I am happy to join Michelle because she knows how to make me laugh, and I would lose a good night's sleep at least once a week for a laugh.

Heath and I bring our glasses inside, and I excuse myself to the bathroom. When I return, I see he's rolled up his sleeves and started scrubbing the pints.

Michelle turns to me, "You can smoke in here if you like."

I've already smoked more cigarettes tonight than I usually do in a month and Heath's story got me thinking it's probably time to quit, but it is a luxury to smoke inside a closed bar so I do.

"I just have to put the money upstairs." Michelle pulls the dishrag out of her pocket. "The padlock is open. I'll meet you two outside."

Heath and I step over the iron-gate and remove the padlock from the door. The street is quiet. It's late. 2:30, maybe 3. Tomorrow, my alarm will go off at 6:30 am and my head and kidneys will ache as I dress the kids in their uniforms, pour Life cereal, and make hummus and pita sandwiches for lunch. But don't think about that yet. You're still standing in the moonlight. The breeze feels cool against your cheeks and the air smells as if it's going to rain, but there's not a cloud in the night sky. Heath walks out grinning with his hands in his pockets, kicking a bottle cap on the ground. He has the kind of ears that make you want to ask, *When did you grow into them?*

"Who's with your kids tonight?" he says.

"My friend. She's sleeping over."

"So you don't have to go home?"

"I always have to go home."

"Is it inappropriate to say that I think you're beautiful and I've enjoyed talking to you?"

I allow myself to receive the compliment. His eyes stay on me, and I hear myself say, "Maybe I don't have to go home just yet."

Michelle slams the gate, then padlocks the door.

"What've you two been conversing about?"

"Juggling," Heath changes the subject.

"I can juggle!" I say too loudly, and I realize I am drunk.

"Seems like you both can," Michelle says, hooking my arm and Heath's.

Michelle waves her hand, and a cab stops. Before I know it, she's guiding me into the back seat. I catch Heath's eye, and as if Michelle feels the exchange go through me, she tightens her grip on my arms. *Ow*. Her eyes shrink to slits. She uses the same tone with me as she did with the busker, "Yer doin great," she says. She gives me a strange, almost threatening look that makes the night replay itself. Then she puts her arm in Heath's and they continue to walk across the street. I roll down the window to hear her infectious laughter. I smell the onions grilling on the street carts while I watch the rest of the night-lovers stumble home.

SUNDAY MORNINGS

On Sundays at 7:45 am, the Road Runners met by the bathrooms on JFK just west of Chain of Lakes Drive in Golden Gate Park. Tanya arrived 15 minutes early to stretch her legs on the kiosk in front of the American bison paddock. It was bizarre seeing these mammoth mammals inside a park instead of thundering across an open plain. These bison were motionless, wallowing in the dirt or standing and chewing grass. She wanted to climb the high fence and pet their shaggy coats, rub their protruding shoulders, and clean the crust out of their tiny brown eyes. No one seemed to care for them. As the fog blew through the eucalyptus trees, she crossed her right leg over her left and folded forward, stretching her IT band. Today was 13 miles.

Tanya started running because every day of her life was someone's worst. She'd treated stab and gunshot wounds. Told families their sons and daughters had died. Stitched up gashes, and prescribed antibiotics for infections. Healed anything from a sprain or fracture to a serious head injury. Ordered hundreds of CTs, EKGs, stress tests, and ultrasounds. And on a rare occasion, delivered a premature baby or assisted a C-section. She used to text Jeff, her boss, and he would meet her in one of the staff rooms. She'd lament about the daily grievances. She'd lock the door and he would hold her. Sometimes she found herself unbuttoning his pants. They'd have sex, then go their separate ways.

To get over Jeff, she depended on wine, Ambien, and Adderall. She didn't want to end up like many of her patients, making up excuses for opiates. So she found something drastic to break her patterns. The coach, Jonathon, blew his whistle and the runners organized themselves by pace. Tanya said hello to the other 10-minute-milers and listened to him explain the route, turnaround points, and water stops. "Remember to share the road," he said. "Don't run with more than two people once we get out of the park. We run on Sundays because there are no cars, but that means more bikes, runners, and kids—so be aware!"

Tanya was acutely aware. She would face the pain. As she began to run, she felt it in her knees, her lower back, and her brain, bouncing in her cranium. Her temples pulsed with pain. She dove into it. *I love pain*, she told herself silently. *The pain will set me free.* Then something strange happened, just as it always did. The pain became background music, calmed by the rhythm of her breath. She stayed in this manageable place for miles, and the world opened up in waves.

Hello, beautiful city! Hello, hummingbird with flapping iridescent wings. Hello, Dutch windmill. Do your blades ever move? Maybe you are broken, but your beauty is not lost. Oooooh...Pacific Ocean! The largest body of water in the world. The edge of the Americas. I can't believe I get to live near you. Move it, asshole. Can you say, on your right? You almost clipped my ankle. Don't you have a bell? Fucking cramp. Go away! One foot in front of the other. It doesn't matter how fast you go. Keep moving forward.

"More than halfway there." Tanya's coach fell back, she knew it was his job to monitor the group and run with people who needed the most support. He ran three marathons a year, keeping his pace under a six-minute mile. It meant he did most of the talking while Tanya nodded. That was the one thing she liked about running: the inability to talk. She hated awkward conversation. Luckily, the 10-minute-milers were solely focused on survival.

"Conserve your energy when you're running into the wind," he told her. "Don't fight it. Slow down your pace a little, then we'll pick it up when we turn around on Sloat." Tanya nodded and looked into his eyes a moment too long. Or did he look into *her* eyes a moment too long? It was hard to tell when jogging and panting. She didn't even know who or what was moving this body. She just felt the rhythm of pain, breath, heartbeat, appreciation, annoyance, self-doubt, fear of failure, motivation, and elation. Repeat.

Tanya knew it was his job to run with the person who looked the most distressed, but she didn't care, she liked running with him. He smelled like oatmeal soap and his breath sounded even and smooth.

"What's your favorite fruit?" he asked, checking to see if she could still talk.

"Cherries," she said. "I...like...ripe cherries."

"In season cherries are the best," he replied. "Try to guess mine. I'll give you a hint. It's both tart and sweet and you can eat the skin."

She looked at him wildly. She feared he'd say kumquat, a fruit she disliked.

"What?" he asked. "You got something against kiwis?"

"Oh...no," she replied, relieved.

"I make a delicious fruit salad with kiwi. You should try it sometime."

When they turned the corner, the wind carried her. She looked at him like, *holy shit*, the Universe was giving her a push. He stayed by her side as they ran back into the park, past the panhandle, down The Wiggle, alongside the Giants' stadium, around the Embarcadero, and up Geary Street to 8th Avenue. He mentioned his sobriety and how running had changed his life. Setting goals and accomplishing things that were impossible for his mind and body to comprehend made the hours easier. "When you quit using," Jonathan said, "there's so much time. I had to fill it with something." He laughed, but she sensed the seriousness of the hours.

Jonathan wanted to see what he could do, not just what he could get away with. The results were incredible: he had a job, a studio apartment, and a car. Things most people took for granted, but he knew they were a gift. He still feared a backslide and socializing wasn't easy for him. He didn't enjoy bars anymore, but his friends were the Road Runners now, and they spent their time outside. Tanya smiled at him, but when her shins hit the hill, she said, "I don't think I can do it. I have to stop."

"Does something hurt?"

"Everything hurts," she said.

He put his hand in his pocket and handed her a Gatorade Gel. She looked at him like he had to be joking. What the hell was that going to do? He mentioned something about being in The Bonk. She looked at him quizzically. "You're hitting a wall," he said. "Your body needs to replenish carbohydrates. If you don't feel injured, this will help you." She wanted to reply, *Those things don't work.* For glycogen to make its way into the muscles, it must first be digested, and it needs time to make its way through the intestinal wall. She could walk to the finish line before that happened. But she couldn't talk. He didn't even know she was a doctor.

"Trust me," he said. "It will wake up your brain." He ripped open the packet.

Tanya put the sugary goo into her mouth and closed her eyes.

"Just imagine your body as a limitless machine."

"And...this...is...unicorn...magic...gas."

"Exactly!" He put the empty packet into his pocket. "Did you know bison can run up to 40 miles an hour?"

Tanya shook her head. "Those...bison...hardly...moved," she replied between heavy breaths. "They live in a cage."

"You can also tell its mood by its tail. If it's standing straight up, it's gonna charge."

Tanya looked at him out of the corners of her eyes.

"I'm from Texas. I know a thing or two about bison."

They made it up the hill and crossed Fulton Street into the park when Tanya felt another wave of energy lift her feet. Was it the goo? It couldn't be. The central governor in her body burned past the fatigue. He picked up the pace, and she found herself keeping up with him. Then he said, "I'll see you at the bison."

Her eyes said, *You can't leave me now*. She didn't want to be alone with the voice that told her she wasn't strong enough. Her sister was the one who was the athlete. She was the one who got good grades. As a kid, she could barely run one loop around the track without heart palpitations. Her body was not meant to do this.

"When you feel like quitting," he said, "think about why you started." And then he took off, blowing past the other runners as if it were his first mile. Tanya hated him. Her heart was in her ears, her skin itched, her inner thighs and bikini line were chaffed. Even if she finished, it was only 13 miles. She'd never be able to make 26. She might as well quit now. She was not a runner.

Tanyla looked up at the trees: blue gum eucalyptus, Monterey pines, oh look, a redwood! They didn't change colors like the trees back home. How could she let go of this sidecar grief if the leaves didn't remind her? She wanted to cry, but her insides were already crying.

Crying for everything she saw on the news. Every day another injustice. Crying for everyone's worst day.

She remembered a story her high school teacher, Mr. Plett, had told her about two frogs hopping into a bucket of buttermilk. Both frogs frantically kicked, yet the struggle became too hard for one, and it gave up while the other persevered. The resilient frog used the hardened butter to jump out and live. *If anything, you are resilient.* With each step, she stomped out the worst. She saw the tall fence that caged the bison. Her tail stood straight up as she charged.

DAYWRECKERS

I need to call home. I walk outside of the hotel room and stand on the balcony overlooking the pool.

"Hi," I say in my hungover voice. "Are the kids up?"

"Yep, watching Little Einsteins."

"I miss them already." I squint into the desert sun. "Did you see the tsunami?"

"Yeah, it's terrible."

"Still think I'm crazy for wanting a disaster plan?"

"I never thought you were crazy, but you can't spend your life this way. What was it last week, Listeria in cantaloupes?"

"Our kids eat cantaloupe all the time. And the San Andreas runs right under our feet. We need to be prepared. Maybe we should move."

"Things can happen anywhere, babe. You can't be ahead of a disaster."

I gaze at the empty pool chairs. I know he is right, but I can't stop the fearful images scrolling in my head.

"How's Palm Springs…how's the *Ace Hotel and Swim Club*?"

"We are the oldest people here."

"I'm sure that's not true."

"No, it has officially happened."

"How was last night?"

"Fine. Everyone just talked about their jobs. Mae is raising venture capital for her clothing line, Kat left Kaiser to go to some boutique hospital, and Fraya is practicing law in Shanghai. She keeps raving about her ayi."

"What's that?"

"Exactly. I have more in common with their nannies now. They keep asking me when I'm going back to work. It makes me feel like a freak."

"You're not a freak. You're a great mom. Please tell Mae happy birthday for me," he says.

"Are you ready for today? They've switched soccer fields, I texted the new location. The birthday party is at four. I told Claire's mom no peanuts. Will you remind her? You'll need to show her how to use the EpiPen. Pack Grace's meds just in case."

"Everyone knows Grace is allergic to peanuts. I'll bring her meds."

"Our disaster meeting place should be in the Presidio. You should get Grace. Jack and I will grab Chloe, and we'll meet beyond Julius Kahn Park."

"Sounds good. We have a plan. Try to have fun."

"It's a shitty day to have fun."

"It's the only day you got."

"You good?" Mae peers over her *Bazaar* magazine that is filled with stickers and notes for her latest fashion collection. All the pool chairs are filled with attractive people, and she looks like one of the models in her fashion ads. She is wearing a multi-colored striped bikini, a wide-brimmed black hat, and aviator sunglasses. Her wrists are circled with gold bangles.

"I think so," I say. I don't tell her that I'm not good. I haven't told anyone. There was a time when these women were my closest friends. We all met in San Francisco when we were single, and we've romanticized the hell out of it ever since.

"You want a drink?" She points to the waitress who is shading my unshaven legs.

"What are you having?" I ask Mae, then smile at the young waitress.

"The Desert Facial. It's good."

I have no idea what the Desert Facial is, but say, "Make that two."

"Three, please," Kat says, adjusting her one-piece bathing suit. It is a modern take on a 1950s style. It is red and backless, with padding to lift up her breasts, stitching to minimize her waist, and it fits like a skirt, so she doesn't even have to wax. She looks stylish yet comfortable, while I suck in, adjust my mismatched suit, and angle my legs.

I recently stopped breastfeeding my eight-month-old son. From far away I might look as if I'm keeping it together, but up close I look like the weird lady at the pool with pubic hair sticking out of my tiny bottoms and an oversized top that my empty flaps of skin no longer fill out.

"Who has the brownies?" Kat sits up.

Mae pulls out the cannabis-infused edibles and unwraps the packaging. Kat eyeballs the brick and cuts it into three exact pieces. "We should eat them at the same time," she says. Kat is a doctor and although I haven't eaten a pot brownie since motherhood, the authoritative tone in her voice gives me the illusion of safety.

"Wait," I say. "I don't know if I should. You know how paranoid I get."

"These are different strains," Kat says. "It's anxiety-reducing."

"Come on," Mae says. "It will be fun. We'll look out for each other."

"Are we sure Freya is okay?" I look at Kat for guidance. Her face is cold, professional with a veneer of empathy. Working in the ER has made her matter-of-fact about tragedy. Years ago, she flew down to New Orleans to help diagnose, bandage, and evacuate the victims of Katrina. Now she stands up to adjust the shade panel over her pool chair, beads of sweat dripping down the backs of her legs. I'm envious of her ability to hold two opposing truths at once; she's able to enjoy beauty while acknowledging the impermanence of it all.

"She's on the phone with the airlines," Mae replies.

"She probably wants to be alone," Kat says. "Her kids and Emmett are fine. The coast of Tohoku is very far from Shanghai. Her fear is understandable, but totally irrational."

I nod my head at her certainty. Mae hands me a piece of brownie and the thick chocolate sticks to my teeth.

"Promise that we check-in on each other?" I say.

"Promise," Mae replies while Kat nods her head.

I feel so out of place at the Ace Hotel that every time the security guard walks near my chair, I casually hold up my hotel wristband like I'm putting a piece of hair behind my ear. Across the pool is a gaggle of 20-something girls, who presumably drove to Palm Springs from LA. They are flawless and tan in neon-colored bikinis and moccasin boots. They have pink zinc oxide under their eyes and down their legs like war paint. They take turns blowing up a lime green inflatable dinosaur. They are so loud and obnoxious that watching them gives me fatigue. Lounging next to the warpaint girls are two hairless bodybuilders in Speedos, who keep rubbing oil on each other's bodies. I can't remember being so romantic that the rest of the world falls away. Surrounding them are pockets of lean guys in ironic trucker hats and multi-colored tattoos who throw a beach ball around the pool to get the attention of the warpaint girls.

The only people I can relate to are a young queer couple with matching short haircuts and a newborn baby. Mom #1 is openly breast-feeding. She looks about my age, somewhere from 28 to 42. Her face is soft and emotionless as her left breast pulses with the rhythm of the baby's sucking. She appears lost somewhere between extreme gratitude and pure exhaustion. I smile at her nostalgically, remembering the time when there was only one baby and you gave yourself up willingly; but when Mom #2 catches my gaze, she misunderstands my look as judgment and narrows her eyes. Mom #1 re-positions her baby higher on her chest and covers her breast with a thin blanket. I almost tell her *No. It's cool. We're also mothers. This is our one weekend away*. But I don't, because not talking about motherhood is a vacation in itself.

So I drop back into the sun chair and have a staring contest with the electric blue sky and the San Joaquin Mountains. I release a yawn. A killer yawn. The yawn I've needed to release for years. Every cell of my body has an influx of oxygen and my restlessness dissolves. I straighten my legs and fold forward, pulling the outside edges of my feet to my face, softening my lower back. Under my left armpit, I can see Mae checking in with me and she doesn't even have to ask, she knows I'm okay. .

I watch the shadows change on the mountain for what seems like hours. Completely content in my aloneness, detached from the three hearts that beat outside my chest. A gate slam behind me. I turn to see an older woman, possibly in her mid-60s, strutting into the pool deck with an inner tube and a jumbo plastic cup from 7-Eleven. She doesn't hesitate stripping down to her turquoise two-piece, her skin hanging like long underwear. She's the only person whose bathing suit is as rundown as mine. I want to befriend her. We are the least glamorous people here. However, without a wristband, I wonder how long it will take before the security guard sniffs her out. I lift my wrist and scratch my nose.

On land, the warpaint girls sit on the lime green dinosaur, two on each hump, they all have their phones..They use them like mirrors. Check their teeth. Fix their hair. Then take selfies. Finally, the girl in the front captures the group.

"Higher," one of them yells, then grabs the phone from her friend. "I look fat. Erase it! Have someone take one of all of us."

One of the trucker guys has found his in. He takes the phone and clicks from every angle.

"I'm so happy we didn't have cameras on our phones," I say to no one in particular.

"That level of self-objectification can't be good for you," Kat replies.

"We didn't have phones," Mae corrects me. "They socialize in completely different ways. They don't know it's offensive."

"Maybe it's not as bad as we think?" I say.

"It's too early to tell," Kat replies.

"Perhaps they're documenting their youth," I shrug.

The new mothers pack up; their motions are quick and their faces are strained. The baby clearly needs a diaper change or to be burped, and the couple hurries to avoid a public meltdown of both mamas and baby. Mae digs her hand into her purse and unwraps the cellophane.

"More?" Mae asks, her eyes lit up.

Doesn't everyone want more?

"Just a smidge," I say, while Mae and Kat eat a whole brownie.

It will be an hour before I know how wrong wanting more will be.

Until then, I watch the warpaint girls straddle the blow-up dinosaur that is still on land. They laugh and dance around it like hedonists. When they finally throw it in, everyone cheers. Hell, I'm cheering until I see Freya walking out of the suite. She is wearing a pressed white shirt, so crisp that I wonder if she's ironed it, and white sunglasses. Her bird legs balancing on wedge sandals. She sits on the end of my chair.

"Any luck with the airlines?" I'm so high that I'm surprised by my ability to speak.

"None." Her nose and cheeks are shell pink from crying.

"I'm so sorry," I say, hoping I sound as sincere as I am, but my voice echoes.

"Vhat's with them?" She replies, in her soft German accent. She points to Mae, whose face is covered by her floppy hat, her ankles turned out like a corpse. Kat is in the fetal position on her side, her red skirt covering her ass.

"We got into the brownies," I say, but Fraya isn't listening.

"It vas a 9.0."

"What?" I don't understand. For a second, I'd forgotten what had happened.

"If I were in Shanghai, I would've flown to Frankfurt to stay with my family. Emmett is too timid to fly with both small children and he thinks it's unnecessary."

"I'm sorry," I say, struggling to get the words out, "but isn't the coast of Tohoku far from Shanghai? I understand not wanting to be so far away, but another aftershock is unlikely, right?"

"Ahhh," she says. "You haven't heard. They announced that a nuclear power plant was damaged. That's why I'm trying to get home. There is no way to tell how far the radiation will go."

She pauses and my mind swirls around the word that makes cancer. I start to feel a pain in my side like something is pecking at me.

"My mother wants Emmett to leave because she remembers Chernobyl."

"Chernobyl." I cough into my elbow like they teach my kids at school.

"Thousands of children were exposed to radiation," she continues. "Shanghai is still very far away but if I were there, I would leave and never have to wonder if five years from now, if they suddenly develop thyroid cancer, it was because Mummy was on holiday with her friends."

I imagine invisible waves creeping under her children's door like smoke. The molecules traveling in all directions, breaking down their cells, damaging their DNA, destroying the innocent without disturbing their sleep. I close my eyes. Anxiety scratches my stomach. It feels like the claws of the baby chicks that jumped on my palm in the incubator at my daughter's preschool. I hear the warpaint girls running on the deck and I watch them cannonball into the pool. A shirtless trucker boy with a tattoo of a puma down his right arm jumps in with his eight-millimeter camera. His arm remains lifted like an ostrich as he tapes the girls giggling and splashing. He pans around the pool, the mountains, and the two palm trees that stretch into the sky like a giant 1980s antenna, then he zooms in on the girls.

"Look at them," Fraya says. "They act like nothing has happened."

My eyes make fake accusations, but aren't we trying to be them?

"There is so much devastation and no one is aware of it," she says.

Two of the warpaint girls attempt to mount the dinosaur that is floating in the pool, but the green monster has a mind of its own. As soon as the girls jump on its back, they fall off howling into the water.

Their neon tops slide down just enough to have everyone watching them; yet, none of them can stay on the dinosaur.

"I don't understand why it's so difficult?" Fraya says dryly. "Maybe they coated it with KY or something? "

"Like the movie Old School."

"Exactly," she smiles. "You don't look well. Maybe you should get out of the heat."

"I'll take a dip," I say, unsure if I can move.

When the camera turns away, I walk down the pool stairs and submerge myself into the cold saltwater, drowning out the squeals of youth and alarms of adulthood. I squinch my eyes and scream underwater. A strange mermaid sound comes out. A watery silence fills my ears as I sink into the part of myself that is constant and childless.

When I pop up, I see the black inner tube. The older lady is so tan that she is purple. She stands in the shallow end with the inner tube around her waist, sucking down her Big Gulp that smells like tequila.

"You think they'd give me a turn on that-there dinosaur?"

"I don't see why not," I say. "Show 'em a thing or two."

"I would if Doofus over here wouldn't throw me out," the lady points to the muscular security guard, and I lift my wrist as if I'm stretching.

"I've been going to this pool longer than he's been alive," she explains. "And he thinks he can stop me? These people slap some paint on a Howard Johnson's and think they're better than everyone else? Once a HoJo, always a HoJo."

"Amen," I say.

"I'm Connie."

"Emma," I reply. "Nice to meet you."

Connie starts telling me some stories about when Frank Sinatra, Kirk Douglas, and Dinah Shore lived here. That's when this place was really cool, she says. She explains that the hostess at the King's Highway diner right inside the Ace used to sing with Sinatra himself.

"If you wanna see something special, she does a mean rendition of Happy Birthday."

"It's my friend Mae's birthday," I say. "That's why we're here."

"Her voice makes the whole diner stop and listen, like a real entertainer, not like the auto-tune-crap-singers of today."

"I'd like to hear that," I say.

"Look at them," Connie points and I get lost in the sky. "It's disgusting! You should see them around five o'clock when they're on top of each other. I don't know why Doofus doesn't kick them out. Damn homos."

"Excuse me?" I ask, loudly. The scratching in my stomach returns. I clutch my side. My tongue swells inside my mouth. The brownie has made it impossible for me to articulate.

"They should be put on their own island," she says.

"I think they're beautiful," is all I can say.

I quickly swim away from Connie and I let the sun dry my body. Fraya sits next to me in a director's chair. She smokes cigarette after cigarette in a chic way that is only possible for Europeans. I grab my phone and scroll. The headline reads, "Power Quake Destroys Northern Japan," and the first image that pops up is a picture of a three-year-old boy. He is clinging to a palm tree, submerged up to his neck in water. No one else is in sight. His nostrils are flared as he looks over his shoulder, presumably for his mother. I let out an audible sigh.

"Are you okay?" Fraya asks, then looks at her phone.

"I didn't eat breakfast," I reply.

"15,000 people were killed," Fraya says, "10,000 people are still missing."

The pain runs to the other side of my stomach. At first, I imagined the pecking to be a fluffy chick. Soft, yellow, and furry, but now I am certain that it is a small brown mouse because I can feel its tail tickling the walls of my digestive organs. It's the same mouse that ran across our kitchen floor and forced my son to jump up on a bar stool. It moves slowly up the maze of my intestines. I tell myself, just like I've told my son, the mouse won't hurt you. Try to remain calm. I don't want to frighten Fraya, who finishes her cigarette, then crosses her arms, and bites her thumbnail. I signal to the waitress.

"You want another?" She yells over the music.

"Water please."

When the waitress hands it to me, I can't decide if I should flush the mouse down or hurl it up. I cough into my elbow, but that only makes the mouse move further up my larynx. I feel my throat closing up. My hands do the universal sign for choking. Where's the security guard when you need him? Why hasn't Mae or Kat checked on me? I thought we were all in this together. Call an ambulance! I put my foot onto Mae's disloyal thigh and shake her awake.

When she sits up, her face is deathly white. Deep worry lines crease her forehead and her chin disintegrates into her neck. She takes off her enormous black hat and covers her face. She must have seen the mouse's tail hanging out of my chapped lips because I hear the daintiest of gags and smell a whiff of gin as she throws up the Desert Facial into her hat.

I cough so hard that the mouse flies out of my mouth and scurries around the pool to the 20-somethings who are making a full-blown documentary. Mae holds the hat filled with regurgitated gin like a serving dish, and we look at each other, bewildered.

"They don't call 'em Daywreckers for nothing," Mae says.

"That's what the brownies were called and you gave them to me?"

"I thought it was just good marketing."

"Oh my God." Freya gets up and walks to the suite or just away from us.

"Don't look," Mae says, "the security guy is headed right for us."

We're getting kicked out of the pool, wristbands or not. Mae stands up and stuffs her hat into the garbage while Connie starts shouting obscenities at the bodybuilders. The security guard looks at us, then at her. Connie runs around the pool in the black inner tube. In one John Wayne-like motion, she drops it on the cement and jumps onto the dinosaur like she's mounting an untamed horse. Her purple-creased thighs hold on for dear life as she grips the black handles and glides into the deep end. Her right hand waves in victory as she shrieks, "Take that, mother-fuckers!" The guy with the eight-millimeter is filming her. The warpaint girls are cheering. The bodybuilders ignore her. Mae is wiping her mouth. Kat may be dead. And I think, *Let go. Let go of the fucking dinosaur.*

READING GUIDE

Theme: OBJECTIFCATION

At one time or another, each of us has faced societal pressures of unattainable body standards. It constantly had me questioning if I felt uncomfortable in my body because something was actually wrong with it or because I was told (by the media or strangers or loved ones) that my body was supposed to look a different way. These stories reflect living in an objectifying culture, and aim to dismantle the false belief that human worth is tied to appearance.

REPRESENTATIVE STORIES

- Put a Teat in It! (p. 1)
- O Youth and Beauty! (p. 3)
- Temporary Thing (p. 50)
- Daywreckers (p. 127)

PROMPTS:

- Write about an environment you've experienced, where body image is extremely important. How did it make you feel?

- Write about a time when your body has rebelled against you. Can you capture a moment of violent change when you no longer felt like 'yourself'?

- Write about a time you felt *animal*.

Theme: HIDDEN WOUNDS

When I wrote "Holy Communion," I had just learned about the Epigenetic Theory–that trauma can leave a chemical mark on a person's genes, which is then passed down to subsequent generations. I had insomnia for most of my childhood, and I coped with it by reading books. Watching my daughter dread sleep without the lived-experiences I had, made me curious if I passed down my unhealed wounds to her. I wanted to face my fears head-on to confront that generational trauma for her, as well as my mother and grandmother.

REPRESENTATIVE STORIES

- Holy Communion (p. 20)
- Saturday Mourning (p. 25)
- Cheap Hotel (p. 108)
- Sunday Mornings (p. 121)
- Daywreckers (p. 127)

PROMPTS:

- What childhood fears keep you up at night?

- What cultural influences inspired your darkest fears?

- Do you carry any secret stories from your family? If so, in which ways have you broken generational trauma?

- Write about a time in your life that you didn't feel in control. What coping mechanisms did you use to come back to yourself and your body?

Theme: ALTERED STATES

In many of the stories, the protagonist is in an altered state due to either recreational drugs, dreams, sleep paralysis, or prescribed medication. I often write about the times when I've experienced altered states that reveal something truer than the reality I've lived. And in that moment of seeing clearly or unclearly, it made me question everything that I accepted as real.

REPRESENTATIVE STORIES

- The Beating (p. 34)
- A Distinguished Man (p. 39)
- Temporary Thing (p. 50)
- AMME (p. 65)
- New Low (p. 99)
- Daywreckers (p. 127)

PROMPTS:

- Write about a time when your consciousness was altered:

  o How did you cope with this new reality?

  o Was it a positive or negative experience or both? What did you learn?

  o Have you been forever altered? If so, what stays with you today?

Theme: LITERATURE AND FILM

Literature and film are used in these stories as means of connection with others. I've felt deep connections with characters in books and desperately needed to discuss them with other people. Even though I'm also a film lover, there is a let down if someone has only seen the movie instead of reading the book. The book gives much more character development and reading is an active engagement. The reader uses their own imagination and becomes a co-creator instead of watching someone else's interpretation. The conversation of their interpretation is what fascinates me. My hope is that readers will be curious about the texts that are mentioned, and will hunt them down like hidden treasures.

REPRESENTATIVE STORIES

- O Youth & Beauty! (p. 3)
- Temporary Thing (p. 50)
- Don't Feed The Pigeons (p. 110)

PROMPTS:

- Read one of the mentioned poems, short stories, or novels and write about the overlapping themes. How do these stories dialogue with older works?

- Read Mary Gaitskill's short story, "Secretary," then watch the 2002 film directed by Steven Shianberg, or read Christopher Isherwood's novel, *A Single Man*, then watch the 2009 film directed by Tom Ford.

o   Write about how the film and literature differ.

  ◊   Did the interpretation of the film surpass the
      literature? If so, how?

  ◊   Did you enjoy one more than the other? If so, why?

ACKNOWLEDGMENTS

This book would not be possible without the editing and love from Sarah Bethe Nelson, who tirelessly read these stories over the last decade. Thank you to my mentor-warrior-hero, Lidia Yuknavitch, for the encouraging words that inspired me to believe in my work. Thank you to the faculty and my MFA community at SF State University. Your brilliance demanded that I worked harder on my craft and I am grateful for it.

Over the last 20 years, there have been so many friends who've been muses to me–you know who you are! And I want to thank you for inspiring me, allowing me to inhabit your world, and giving me much liberty with your narratives. Special shout out to my larger-than-life friends, Amme Hill and April Pride, for always expanding and being true to yourself.

Much appreciation to J. K. Fowler for believing in this collection and giving it a home at Nomadic Press. I deeply enjoyed the process of editing this book, and that's because of Michaela Mullin of Nomadic Press, who spent countless hours editing and preparing this book for the world. A big thank you to my artist friend and overall generous human, Sarah Farrell Mackessy, for creating this beautifully complicated collage art for the cover. And many thanks to Jevohn Tyler Newsome for the book design.

Finally, the warmest thank you to my beloved family (aka the three hearts that beat outside my chest) and husband for loving and supporting me. And to my mother for giving me life and always supporting my creativity.

Additionally, I'd like to thank the following journals and publications for giving earlier versions of these stories a home:

—◈—

"Put a Teat In It" won the *Los Angeles Review* Flash Fiction award, 2020.

"New Low" won the Nomadic Press Bindle Award, 2018.

"Holy Communion" was published in *Entropy*, March 2020, and was first-runner up for the *Los Angeles Review* Non-Fiction Award, 2017.

"Saturday Mourning" was published in *Cosmonauts Avenue* and won the Leo Litwak Award, 2015.

"The Beating" was published in *Midnight Breakfast* and *Mutha Magazine*, 2016.

"My Collection" was published in *sPARKLE & bLINK*, 2014.

Jennifer Lewis

Jennifer Lewis is a writer, editor, and publisher of Red Light Lit. In 2020, she won the *Los Angeles Review* Flash Fiction Award for "Put a Teat in It." In 2018, her short story, "New Low," was the winner of the Nomadic Press Bindle Award and in 2017, she was the first runner-up for the *Los Angeles Review* Creative Nonfiction Award for "Holy Communion." Her fiction has been published in *Cosmonaut's Avenue*, *ENTROPY*, *Fourteen Hills Press*, *The Los Angeles Press*, *Midnight Breakfast*, *sPARKLE & bLINK*, and *X-Ray Lit Mag*. She received her MFA in creative writing from San Francisco State University in May 2015. She teaches at The Writing Salon in San Francisco.

COVER MISSIVE

by Sarah Farell

Having explored the art of collage and assemblage for the past 25 years I am guided and intrigued by relationships between disparate elements. My technique intersects traditional cut & paste methods with graphic digital design. When entering into collective creation, I pull inspiration from my background in devised theatre and circus/clown art. Work creation with a manuscript begins with a set of guiding words that help to expose the core essence of a story, or set of stories.

In the case of Jennifer Lewis' collection *The New Low*, she provided me with the following guiding words: Tsunami, Mountains, Antenna Palm Trees, Sunshine, Pool. I used these guiding words to begin creating multiple design options before I read her works in order to avoid the trap of being too literal.

Nomadic Press Emergency Fund

Nomadic Press Black Writers Fund

Right before Labor Day 2020 (and in response to the effects of COVID), Nomadic Press launched its Emergency Fund, a forever fund meant to support Nomadic Press-published writers who have no income, are unemployed, don't qualify for unemployment, have no healthcare, or are just generally in need of covering unexpected or impactful expenses.

Funds are first come, first serve, and are available as long as there is money in the account, and there is a dignity centered internal application that interested folks submit. Disbursements are made for any amount up to $300.

All donations made to this fund are kept in a separate account. The Nomadic Press Emergency Fund (NPEF) account and associated processes (like the application) are overseen by Nomadic Press authors and the group meets every month.

On Juneteenth (June 19) 2020, Nomadic Press launched the Nomadic Press Black Writers Fund (NPBWF), a forever fund that will be directly built into the fabric of our organization for as long as Nomadic Press exists and puts additional monies directly into the pockets of our Black writers at the end of each year.

Here is how it works:

$1 of each book sale goes into the fund.

At the end of each year, all Nomadic Press authors have the opportunity to voluntarily donate none, part, or all of their royalties to the fund.

Anyone from our larger communities can donate to the fund. This is where you come in!

At the end of the year, whatever monies are in the fund will be evenly distributed to all Black Nomadic Press authors that have been published by the date of disbursement (mid-to-late December).

The fund (and associated, separate bank account) has an oversight team comprised of four authors (Ayodele Nzinga, Daniel B. Summerhill, Dazié Grego-Sykes, and Odelia Younge) + Nomadic Press Executive Director J. K. Fowler.

Please consider supporting these funds. You can also more generally support Nomadic Press by donating to our general fund via nomadicpress.org/donate and by continuing to buy our books.

As always, thank you for your support!

Scan the QR code for more information and/or to donate.

You can also donate at nomadicpress.org/store.